Differences

Differences

It is not the shade of one's skin that defines a person,

but how he is as a human being.

Cristina Monro

PARTRIDGE

A Penguin Random House Company

To order additional copies of this book, contact
Toll Free 800 101 2657 (Singapore)
Toll Free 1 800 81 7340 (Malaysia)
orders.singapore@partridgepublishing.com

www.partridgepublishing.com/singapore

Chapter

1

New York was Cara Marino's kind of city. To New York's regular habitues, it was just their ordinary city, nothing to wax romantic about, but not to a movie buff like Cara. New York to her was the choiced setting of many cinematic romances.

An unexpected spectacle met her when their plane descended towards the JFK Airport runway. A sunset. God's masterpiece from His divine palette gilded the sky in a burst of orange and gold, celebrating the day's final fanfare. New York never failed to move her, especially Manhattan, the city's core, which she found beguiling and exciting. The days were inching towards the end of the year, and another year was poised to herald its entry.

The queue at Immigration was long. A curt Immigration officer addressed the seventy-ish female Asian traveler ahead of Cara who was struggling with her minimal English. Cara assessed her as a Chinese mother travelling alone, perhaps for the first time to visit a New York-based son or daughter. She was obviously rattled by the impatience of the Immigration officer. A Chinese youth in the next lane came to the rescue and translated it into Mandarin. What a pathetic sight. How sad that to gain entry to this proverbial land of milk and honey, people of other races became prey to humiliation, Cara mused.

A position awaited her at the United Nations Development Programme as senior writer in the Media Relations Office on a one-year renewable contract. She responded to the job opening through the internet and was readily accepted. Her extensive work experience plus a Master's degree in Communication, *cum laude*, earned from Fordham U served her well. At 25, when most of her friends in the Philippines were raising families, marriage was the least of her priorities, to her parents' chagrin. Her sense of adventure had not yet peaked. The U.N. job beckoned, and she loved New York.

As she emerged with her luggage, there was her cousin Melissa waving frantically. She was a year older than Cara, and they were the best of cousins.

"I can't believe you're finally here," said Melissa, hugging her. "Maybe now we can find you a suitable partner."

Melissa was married to an American and they had a cute three-year-old daughter they named Francine, who was Cara's godchild. Melissa hoped that her cousin would somehow follow the same marital path.

"Melissa, please give me time to breathe and get settled. I'm not here to hunt for a boyfriend. You know that."

"But it would be nice if you can find a boyfriend. Cara, you're 25 years old!"

The audible statement from Melissa attracted glances from the other travelers, who, like them, were pushing their baggage carts towards the exit.

"I found you a nicely furnished studio flat in midtown Manhattan with a reasonable lease after haggling with the landlord. The Asian in me – haggle, haggle," Melissa bragged. "It's just a single ride on Bus 106 to the U.N. I'm quite positive you'll love it."

"Thanks a lot, Melissa. I owe you. That saves me a lot of trouble, and I trust your taste."

The apartment was on the third floor and just a few blocks walk to the bus route. Cara was immediately drawn to its aura. She liked the furnishings done predominantly in beige with a touch of maroon. It was a one-room affair, yet the architect did not seem to have scrimped on space despite its being just a studio apartment. It was bigger than what Cara expected. The living-dining-kitchen scenario was spacious enough, not cramped and claustrophobic. The bedroom area had a sliding panel, which isolated it from the rest of the flat and gave it some privacy. To top it all, the lease was within the limit she was entitled to in her U.N. position. Melissa provided the apartment with bedsheets, towels, a few pieces of chinaware and cutlery, so all Cara had to do was move in.

"How did you find this?," she asked Melissa with a trace of excitement in her voice.

"You know me. I'm a certified bargain hunter. Keith always credits me for that."

"Hey, how's that cute hubby of yours, by the way?"

"You know what? I must be a good cook because he's starting to develop a paunch."

"Oh, no. Prince charming with a belly?," she teased Melissa.

"Don't worry. We'll find you one with great abs."

"There you go again, Melissa. You're impossible."

Chapter

2

If Cara's parents had their way, they would never have allowed her to work in New York. In her country, parents were overly protective towards their children, especially with their daughters. Cara had a promising job back home, and she led a sheltered life. Although she did not consider her family wealthy, like the reigning Spanish and Chinese families dominating most businesses, they lived comfortably. Her father was CEO of an Italian company. They resided in a well-guarded and decent subdivision in the heart of Makati, Manhattan's equivalent, with a family driver and a coterie of domestic help to attend to their needs. She and her brother went to exclusive schools and had the chance to travel during school breaks. Her family was able to afford to send them abroad for postgraduate studies.

They were brought up properly, and their parents never eased up in their parental responsibility of instilling in them the right values. They grew up in an atmosphere of love and freedom to express their opinions. Cara reasoned out to her parents that her lackluster job in a top corporation was no longer fulfilling to her, and the position at the U.N. came as her option at an opportune time. She could not just let this slip through her fingers without at least giving it a try.

Back home, a daughter was never too old to be the recipient of constant reminders from her parents on proper behavior befitting a lady.

The examples Filipino mothers set for their daughters, and their words of caution, which somehow became a subtle brain-washing ritual, compelled their girls to preserve their virginity until they were ready for marriage. Filipinos put a premium on virginity, and most Filipino men still prefer to marry virgins. Cara received her parents' blessings after a series of heart-to-heart talks with them. Her parents' initial reluctance was partly borne out of a selfish reason of having her close by and not a continent away from them.

Her parents' love story was something lifted from a movie script. Her father was sent to the Philippines as an expatriate to look into his company's business in the country. In one of his trips to the south, he met Cara's mother and fell in love with her instantly. Her mom was from a respectable family and at that time was bethrothed to a scion of a well-to-do family there. The romantic Italian won the heart of the southern lass. He asked his company to assign him permanently in the Philippines, a country which he learned to love. His base became Makati City in Metro Manila, where Cara and her older brother Vince were born.

* * *

Cara relished the walk to the bus stop in the crisp morning air. One of her dreams was to walk through a canopy of trees in a rainforest where light filtered through the branches. She considered the beauty of a rainforest as nature's gift. New York's skyscrapers were her only "trees" right now. She stopped by a corner stand to buy a bagel and coffee for her breakfast. There was already a queue of five office workers in corporate attire.

"You want cream cheese on your bagel?," the man at the stand asked in his heavy Italian accent, which Cara found cute and reminded her of her Italian father. Two women, probably his wife and daughter, assisted him in this bun-on-the-run business. It seemed to be doing briskly because as Cara glanced back, the number of people behind her had doubled in a minute.

"Yes, please, but not too much," Cara replied. She carried her breakfast in a brown bag to the bus stop where she waited for her ride.

* * *

Cara expected security to be strict at the U.N., and she could understand why by the very nature of their work. The security guard took five minutes to go through her papers meticulously. She was to report to Mr. Alec Stevenson, director of Media Relations. His office was on the fifth floor of the UNDP Building on 45th Street, across the main U.N. landmark edifice characterized by its façade of colorful flags of various nations waving at the wind's whim.

It was 8:15 in the morning, and the guard manning the fifth floor said that people report for work at 9:00. Cara quietly ate her breakfast in one corner of the waiting area while reading a copy of the New York Times she picked up earlier when she got down from her bus. She had time to do the crossword puzzle. Despite her adeptness in solving one, she found their version extremely challenging and oftentimes difficult to complete.

Alec Stevenson, an Englishman in his early fifties, was endowed with a jovial personality. Cara liked him at first meeting. His firm handshake and smile could be considered positive indications, and he made her feel at ease.

"You certainly look younger than what it says in your resume," he commented.

"Asians usually look younger than their age, Mr. Stevenson," Cara explained. "I don't know if it's because of our tropical climate or just genetics."

"That's interesting. You can call me Alec. We're on first-name basis in this office. We want everybody to feel comfortable working here."

Alec briefed her on the scope of her work and the responsibilities of their office. The Media Relations group managed the publicity made accessible to the tri-media: print, radio, and television. Press releases normally originated from their office. This was where they were written, edited, and issued. They also needed to constantly monitor the news affecting the U.N. to ensure that there was fair and accurate reporting. Alec continued to dwell on the intricacies of publicity work on a global perspective. Cara realized that their audience was not restricted to U.S. media, and her knowledge could, in fact, contribute to how the press releases were formulated by employing her Asian orientation when called for. Current U.N. issues were more focused on Asia, such as poverty, population, nuclear power, water, environment, food shortage, human rights violation, women's rights, and war. Name it - Asia has it, as one of the staff described the formidable range of issues in this continent, and they were right along UNDP's alley.

Georgia, Alec's African-American secretary, directed Cara to her cubicle. Alec was the only one with a room of his own. Cara found her assigned cubicle agreeable. It was open, meaning doorless, well-lit, having a window with a view of the adjacent building and a partial view of the U.N. landmark. She had this habit of looking out the window while writing, sometimes to draw some inspiration, or simply to temporarily break the tedium of work. The view this one offered was pleasant enough for her.

Georgia introduced her to the other people in the office who were of varied nationalities. She immediately sensed the cohesiveness of the group. During lunch break, she went with Georgia for lunch at the UNDP cafeteria, which served a variety of food choices. Aside from the usual American food, it also had Mexican, Italian, Japanese, Indian, and Chinese. Cara opted for a generous serving of pasta with pesto sauce which came with two slices of Italian bread. Lisa, Valerie, and Ramon from the same office whom she met earlier, joined their table. Lisa and Ramon were writers like her, although Cara's position was a rung higher since she was more senior, and Valerie was a secretary. Only Georgia was married. Cara shared about herself. None of them had been to any part of Asia. They were unanimous in rating Alec as a considerate boss, and Georgia attested to it. Thank my lucky stars, Cara thought privately. She believed that the worst thing that could happen to her was to have a difficult boss in a new job on foreign soil.

Chapter

3

"Have you heard of Daniel Devereaux?," Alec asked Cara as he entered her cubicle. He was wearing a colorful necktie with the print of a cartoon character, the Tasmanian Devil, on it. She smiled in private as she caught a glimpse of it, not expecting Alec to wear something stylish and boyish. He seated himself in one of her chairs.

"Vaguely. I seem to keep hearing that name, even on the bus this morning. Is he a movie star or someone from show biz perhaps? The name certainly sounds like one."

"No. Daniel Devereaux anchors the top-rated talk show *Pulse* at Global Communications Network. The show is consistently No. 1 in the Nielsen ratings for its category. It recently won the Emmy for Outstanding Interview and Interviewer, edging out *Larry King Live, 20/20,* and *60 Minutes*, and the show is comparatively new. Many credit its dynamic anchor for the show's popularity. Daniel Devereaux has charisma, and the program has an excellent format. *Pulse* is a well put-together program with relevant issues and a line-up of very important and interesting guests."

"Earlier, we received an invitation for the Secretary-General to guest in the show. *Pulse* wants to delve into the existing situation in China, particularly the human rights issue, and focus on the U.N.'s initiatives. The Office of the Secretary-General is asking us to handle the pre-show requirements from our end since UNDP is immersed with the ongoing situation there. Our role is to assist GCN in the editing plus seeing to it that they have the right facts. I'm assigning you to this project, Cara. You'll be working closely with Devereaux and his group maybe just for a day or two. I'll be available in case you'll need my assistance. I'll ask Georgia to lend you the materials we have on China which will give you a clearer picture. This is highly sensitive, and this is where your communication skills will come to the fore. Well, what do you say?" Alec flashed her his familiar grin.

"Wow, it sounds exciting," Cara remarked.

"That's the spirit!"

"What's the first step?"

"Tomorrow morning we'll both go to GCN. They've scheduled an initial small-group discussion with Devereaux's team and us. The meeting will be at 10:00, so we'll leave here at around 9:30."

It was just her second day at UNDP and Cara already felt that the challenges were not slow in coming. This was the pace she favored where she was kept on her toes, but not necessarily overworked. Just then Georgia came in with folders and discs.

"Alec said you'll be needing these," laying them on Cara's desk.

"Thanks, Georgia."

"My, my, so you'll be working with Daniel Devereaux. My dear, the guy is a bachelor, one of the most eligible in New York. A lot of women must be dying to be in your shoes," Georgia revealed excitedly.

"Really? He seems to have quite a reputation. What does the man have?"

"He's devastatingly handsome, my dear, and he's 32 years old."

"And single? You're positive he's not gay?"

"Definitely not. He's very *macho* and has had a lot of girlfriends. I brought you this magazine which featured him so you'll have an idea."

Georgia showed Cara a write-up on Daniel Devereaux. It linked him with four women – an actress, a news anchor from another network, a model, and a producer from his own network. There were photos of him escorting each of the women. The write-up was entitled *Oh, Danny Boy*, which Cara found amusing.

"He's good-looking all right. Now my curiosity is challenged. Tell you what, Georgia, after our meeting tomorrow, I'll give you a rundown and my assessment of Daniel Devereaux."

"That's your assignment, Cara," Georgia retorted with a laugh. "Maybe we can meet for lunch at the cafeteria? Valerie and Lisa will want to join us."

After Georgia's exit, Cara could not help smiling to herself. She was intrigued by this man who could create such a stir, especially among the women. Alec also regarded him in a positive way from a masculine standpoint.

Cara turned her attention to the materials on her desk. She picked up the file on top and scanned the pages. She had much to learn about China. She was aware that it was a country where women were subordinated. Could she live in that kind of environment?, she wondered. She was brought up to be assertive and independent, so maybe not. To her, the violation of human rights was downright unChristian, and she happened to be Catholic.

Chapter

4

Alec and Cara arrived at the GCN headquarters fifteen minutes early. A GCN staff ushered them into the conference room, and while they made their way, heads turned momentarily towards them. She caught a hint of a condescending smirk from one of the women, a tall and attractive blonde with heavy make-up who gave Cara a head-to-toe appraisal. Cara was not one who could easily be put down by a mere look. She was wearing a becoming navy blue blazer and mini skirt which showed off her great figure and shapely legs. Her make-up was minimal, something she could get away with. There can only be one possible reason, she thought, and that is because I am not Caucasian. Cara's features attested to her having a half-Asian, half-Italian parentage. She had her father's dark Italian features manifested in her dark brown hair and eyes, and her Filipino mother's complexion and willowy figure. The men, on the other hand, cast her a look of admiration. Cara's looks were uncommon even in a city of convergence like New York. She had flawless light olive skin like a natural tan, which was the envy of many. She could be the odd one since she neither looked Caucasian nor Asian. She was actually Eurasian, a raving product of the fusion of disparate genes.

The conference room had a seating capacity for 20 people and surrounded by windows. Alec and Cara were the first to arrive and were immediately drawn to the magnificent view of the city from the GCN Building. They stood gazing through the window in admiration when they heard the sound of muffled footsteps, prompting them to turn around and come face to face with the imposing figure of Daniel Devereaux. He walked towards them and extended his hand.

"Good morning. I'm Daniel Devereaux. Thank you for coming." His voice was a deep baritone, an anchor's asset. Then he introduced David Marsh, executive producer; Victor Falco, head of the video group; and Josh Green, senior writer. They formed the *Pulse* lead team.

"Hi, I'm Alec Stevenson. This is Cara Marino, our senior writer."

"How do you do, Miss Marino." Daniel Devereaux took Cara's extended hand in a firm grip, and she acknowledged his greeting, giving him a warm smile. His piercing green eyes looked deeply into her own. He was exceptionally tall. At 5'8", she was considered tall for a female in her country, and she was practically looking up at him. He had a good head of brown hair with no receding hairline in view, and a trim masculine physique. Overall, he was striking. He wore a gray suit with a purple shirt underneath and a tie a shade lighter. Very sophisticated, Cara judged his sartorial taste. He moved with confidence and elan, which were not studied but something innately him. When Alec addressed him as "Mr. Devereaux", he stressed "Please call me Daniel."

They took their seats in the oblong conference table. Cara sat beside Alec, and Daniel took the seat facing Alec.

As executive producer, David Marsh explained: "We have existing footages which we want you to look at. These are fairly recent. Victor here was on a mission to China only last month, and he and his crew were able to capture some scenes which may be relevant to our interview."

Victor checked the VCR and played the tape. It was a fifteen-minute run. Some scenes of China depicted human behavior which could be used as visuals for the interview, Alec and Cara both agreed.

"The footages may not show outright human rights violations," Daniel admitted.

"We know it's actually happening there," Alec added. "The U.N. is deeply concerned about the situation in China, and the Secretary-General agreed to this interview. We would like Cara to assist you in the editing. She has extensive writing and editing experience, and she's Asian. She can report here tomorrow and work with you on the script. How does that sound to you?"

"That's fine with us," Daniel replied, turning his head slightly to face Cara wth a serious expression. Cara observed that he never smiled. During their one-hour meeting, not once did he smile. He was definitely very good-looking, "devastatingly" was Georgia's adverb. His maleness was somewhat frightening to Cara, and it could be disconcerting to a woman like her.

After exiting from the conference room, the blonde, who earlier gave Cara the lookover, approached Daniel Devereaux and linked her arm with his possessively.

"Pretty blonde. Must be his girlfriend," Alec whispered to Cara.

* * *

Back at the office over lunch, Georgia, Valerie, and Lisa awaited with bated breath Cara's glowing accounts of the meeting. Over chicken *enchilada*, Cara described Daniel Devereaux to them.

"He's everything that you told me, perhaps even more. I can't blame the women for flocking to him if you say he's eligible. He's impeccably dressed. Overall, he's very attractive, although I detect some arrogance because he doesn't smile, but he can really take your breath away. There was this blonde who behaved like she's more than an acquaintance to him."

"That must be Madeline Foster," Georgia butted in. "She's a producer in one of the shows at GCN. She and Daniel Devereaux have been seen dating. She's one of those women in that article I showed you. As far as she's concerned, she has already marked him with her personal tattoo."

Chapter

5

The office of *Pulse* was one large room with two private rooms within it, one for Daniel and another one for David. Five of the staff were already there when Cara arrived, Victor among them. He and Cara went through the footages again and they rated the scenes according to their relevance. When Josh arrived, they discussed the script. A few minutes later, David came in. There was immediate rapport among the four of them, and Cara was thankful for that.

"We'll show the draft of the script to Daniel as soon as he arrives. He has a sharp eye and he may be able to spot something we missed," Josh said.

"Is he meticulous?," Cara asked.

"You think I'm meticulous?" Daniel Devereaux strode into the office, obviously overhearing their conversation.

"Good morning," Cara said with a smile. She was not prepared to say anything else at the moment. She smelled the manly scent of his cologne. Today he was in a brown suit, which complemented his hair color.

"Good morning, Miss Marino," he replied with a straight face. "I hope everything is in order at the start of your day with us."

"The name is Cara, Mr. Devereaux. My day is starting just fine. Thank you."

"Good to hear that. Everybody calls me Daniel here." He went into his office briefcase in hand, leaving the door ajar, and they could hear him making phone calls.

For the entire morning over a cup of coffee, Josh and Cara reviewed the draft. Cara gave her suggestions, while sharing with him her knowledge of Chinese culture and idiosyncrasies. Some light moments resulted in chuckles. Daniel must have wondered what was going on because he gave a furtive glance in their direction through the glass panel in his office. The most vital facets of the script were the questions Daniel would ask the Secretary-General. These were what Josh and Cara were formulating, but Daniel would have his own questions and the final say.

Just before lunchtime, the blonde Madeline walked in. She proceeded directly to Daniel's room, and closed the door behind her, leaving a trail of strong perfume along her path. The guys looked at each other knowingly, and Cara felt left out for a brief second.

Before noon, David invited them for lunch at the Chinese restaurant on the next block. His treat, he said, to sort of give them a feel of China. At the entrance of the restaurant was a conspicuous sign which said "No MSG". Cara was relieved because monosodium glutamate seemed to have an after-effect on her. It was a fairly decent Chinese restaurant, small and cozy. They chose a corner table for four, and Cara picked the seat against the wall. Typical of Chinese tradition, the interior was done in red with Chinese characters dominating its décor. The waitress wearing a *cheongsam*, the traditional Chinese dress, served them tea initially. They referred to it as the "house brew". They made separate choices from the menu. Cara ordered the chicken with cashew nuts. Just then, Madeline entered the restaurant with Daniel in tow.

"Don't look now, but the dragon queen just made her entrance with our Daniel," Josh announced discreetly.

Daniel noticed them and nodded his head. They took the table on the opposite corner. Since she was directly facing the pair, Cara could not help but notice Madeline constantly touching Daniel's arm and hand, a possessive gesture which seemed to proclaim they were lovers.

"Are the two?…you know," Cara asked, putting her two index fingers together to indicate a relationship.

"Nah," David was quick in answering.

"Daniel doesn't seem to have any serious romantic involvement. Occasional flings maybe," Josh added.

"Women are actually doing the chasing because he's a good catch. He's good-looking and successful," Victor contributed. "Right, David? You and Daniel are buddies."

"I've known Daniel since Columbia U days. We discovered we're a lot alike in many ways. We both have conservative tastes when it comes to women. That explains why the two of us haven't settled down yet," David said with a grin. "Daniel doesn't go much for the flirty, clinging type. I guess he's just dating Madeline. She can be persistent, you know."

"The dragon queen sinks her claws," Josh said in a guttural tone demonstrating with his fingers bent in attack.

"Be careful, he might hear you," Cara warned, stealing a glance at the pair. This time Madeline was whispering into Daniel's ear.

"Who, Daniel?," Josh replied. "He's one of the guys. You can say practically anything to him."

"He doesn't strike me as the friendly type."

"You should get to know him, Cara. He's really a great guy. He's brilliant and kind-hearted, a good combination if you ask me. Trust me," David assured her.

"It's a pleasure working with Daniel. He has this boyish enthusiasm that's contagious," Josh added. "You can get drawn to his zest and drive."

"Yeah, and when he gets fired up with something, we get carried away, too," Victor quipped in.

After their meal, the waitress brought in a tray of fortune cookies. They cracked open their cookies simultaneously to take out their written fortunes.

"This is the best part of a Chinese meal. I get a kick out of reading my fortune from a cookie, even if I don't really believe what it says," Josh confessed.

"Mine says, *'Listen to your heart and balance it with reason'*," Cara read. "Well, that sounds sensible enough."

"What's this? The words don't make any sense at all. It's all garbled," Victor complained, running his fingers through his thinning pate.

"Victor, English is not their language. You mustn't expect the Chinese to be fluent in it," Cara explained. It elicited a laugh from the guys, which attracted Daniel's glance.

They had to pass by Daniel's table on their way out of the restaurant. Cara avoided looking at the pair. David touched Daniel on the shoulder before exiting.

"Who's that woman?," Cara overheard Madeline questioning Daniel, but she did not catch his reply.

* * *

Daniel got back to the office fifteen minutes after they had arrived and posted himself in the large room with the rest of them. Sitting casually on the edge of Josh's desk and having discarded his coat, he read the draft, scribbled some notes on the margins and discussed a few points with them. He was quite objective, and he listened intently to their views and suggestions. In the midst of their discussion, he abruptly turned to Cara.

"As a TV viewer, what is your assessment of *Pulse*?"

"To be honest with you, I've never watched it. I arrived in the U.S. only this week, and the program is not aired in my country." Cara was slightly flattered that he asked her opinion.

"We can take care of that. Victor can show you the tapes of past interviews. Maybe we can start with the last one."

The most recent interview was with the administrator of the Environmental Protection Agency. It focused on the country's current environmental issues and touched on pollution, global warming, and genetically modified food. Cara was impressed with the way Daniel conducted the interview. His questions were relevant and demanded answers the public would want to hear. She expressed her impressions to him, and he seemed satisfied. She learned from the staff that Daniel also hosts *Updates,* a weekly program, but his daily program *Pulse* was his main thing.

* * *

Daniel Robert Devereaux was every woman's fantasy. His dashing good looks, his being a highly popular TV personality, and the fact that he was a bachelor, gave women the dogged determination in their relentless pursuit to snare him for a husband. Women's circles in New

York casting votes among themselves were unanimous in rating him as the most eligible bachelor of their city. Aside from his prestigious Emmy Award, he was voted by People Magazine as one of the sexiest men alive. One would be inclined to expect that all the accolades heaped on Daniel would transform him into a swell-head, but Daniel Devereaux was of a rare breed. He never wanted to call attention to himself, and he shunned publicity. He had been linked to a number of lovely women, but none of them seemed to merit becoming Mrs. Daniel Devereaux by his personal criterion. His friends teased and cajoled him about his status, but he just shrugged them off.

"What are you waiting for, Daniel?," a GCN executive taunted him. "You're ripe for marriage."

"In time. I'm old-fashioned when it comes to that," he replied.

"An old-fashioned playboy? You're an oxymoron, Daniel."

"Whatever you say, but I believe marriage is a serious matter. I'm not a proponent of divorce, so making the right choice is important to me," he justified.

Chapter

6

It was Saturday, Cara's first weekend in New York. She woke up late and started preparing her breakfast of cereal, toast, and coffee when the phone rang. It was Melissa checking up on her.

"Hey, how was your week? I tried calling you at UNDP but all I got was your answering machine, and you didn't return my calls," Melissa whined.

"I'm sorry, Melissa. I forgot to check my phone messages. I wasn't at UNDP for the rest of the week because Alec assigned me to Global Communications Network. The Secretary-General will be interviewed on television, and I was asked to help with the editing of the script."

"Wow, you're busy already. Where is he appearing?"

"In *Pulse*."

"Hey, that's Daniel Devereaux's program."

"Right."

"That handsome anchor is a bachelor, Cara," she said with emphasis.

"So? What are you thinking, Melissa?"

"Don't you find him attractive? Did you get to meet him? What's he like in person?"

"One question at a time, Melissa," Cara cautioned. "Yes, he's very good-looking, and I met him, but he doesn't smile. The people at the network like him, and they swear he's a great guy. He might as well be the *ang principeng hindi tumatawa* (the prince who does not smile). Remember that legend in Filipino when we were in grade school?"

"He's a prince all right. You're one lucky girl. Say, if you're free tomorrow, why don't you have lunch here? I'll pick you up at ten. You can spend the day here, and we can talk. We've a lot to catch up on. What say you?"

"Okay. I'm looking forward to seeing your family again."

* * *

Towards the afternoon, after Cara had dusted and cleaned her place, she decided to take a walk and look for a bookstore to browse. She was a wide reader and she was never without a book to read. She had just finished reading *One Hundred Years of Solitude* by Gabriel Garcia Marquez. She ran a brush through her hair of below-the-shoulder length and put on a white T-shirt, fitting denim pants, a black blazer, and black high-cut leather shoes.

The Barnes & Noble bookstore near St. Patrick's Cathedral had several patrons that early afternoon, and none of its aisles was empty. She checked the bestseller counter and leafed through a couple of new ones. Then she looked at the wide selection of cookbooks. She saw one on one-dish meals and was tempted to get it, but decided to put it down for later. As she moved to the humor section, she picked up Bill Cosby's *Time Flies* and read the first page. She found it hilarious and stifled a laugh. She knew her father would like it, and got it for him. She remembered one particular book she had been wanting to read, *Daughter of Fortune* by Isabel Allende. She scanned the fiction section where the books were alphabetically arranged by author. There it was on the top shelf. She tiptoed to get it and felt a hand brush against hers reaching for the same book. She turned to see who beat her to it and looked directly into a pair of green eyes.

"Here." It was Daniel Devereaux handing her the book. He was in casual attire, beige cargo pants, and plaid shirt with rolled-up sleeves. He did not seem intimidating in his nonexecutive look.

"Thanks. I've been meaning to get this," she told him.

"Do you do much reading?"

"Whatever time I can get. How about you, do you come here often?"

"Bookstores are my regular haunts."

"Me, too. I can lose myself in a bookstore," she revealed with a smile. "I sometimes order through the internet. There's less hassle, but it robs you of the pleasure of browsing in a bookstore," he admitted.

"I know the feeling," she agreed without hesitation.

There was a slight pause, although not awkward in nature, and neither of them uttered a word. They just stared at each other for a brief second until Daniel broke the silence.

"By the way, I haven't formally thanked you for helping us with the editing. You made our work easier."

"It was part of my job assignment. I found it challenging, and I met new and interesting people. You've got quite a team there."

"Yes, it's a hard-working and dedicated team all right."

"Well, I should be getting along and pay for these books. Have a nice day."

"You, too."

As she walked away from him, somehow she could feel his eyes on her back, scrutinizing her and watching her move. She dismissed it as just her imagination. Maybe she just wanted him to look at her, she told herself. When she got to several paces farther, she looked back and saw him looking at her, and she smiled. He did not smile back, but made a small wave of his hand. Daniel Devereaux liked to watch Cara Marino walk, and he found her attractive.

Chapter

7

Spending Sunday with Melissa and her family was a welcome respite. Home to them was a two-story suburban house in Stamford, Connecticut, just a short drive from New York City. It was an old house which they remodeled. Keith Matthews was an architect and had done wonders to the place. After the reconstruction work, the former owners of the house failed to recognize it. It was like a person who underwent a massive facelift and emerged with a totally new face.

Country scenes evoked a touch of sentimental softness in Cara. Time seemed to stand still, and everything was in slow motion. She played with Francine in the yard, then she and Melissa had their tete-a-tete while Keith was barbecuing. It was the tail end of summer, and autumn was preparing to announce its presence. Cara was looking forward to experiencing autumn again which she referred to as 'the nostalgic season'. If spring turns man's fancy into thoughts of love, autumn weaves poetry into the poignant chamber of man's soul.

An hour after their satisfying lunch, while they rested in the veranda, Cara drifted into a *siesta* while sitting in the rocking chair. She dreamed of Daniel Devereaux. She was walking down a country road. He appeared riding a black stallion and blocked her path. In a menacing voice he told her, 'Give me my book.' She answered him, 'What book?' He dismounted from his horse and held her by the shoulders saying 'The book you took from me.' Cara woke up with Melissa's hands on her shoulders.

"Cara, were you dreaming? You were moaning a little."

"That's funny. I was dreaming of Daniel Devereaux accusing me of stealing his book. It must be because I bumped into him in the bookstore yesterday and we were both buying books."

"Dreaming of Daniel Devereaux? Cara, that means you're thinking of him subconsciously."

"I don't think so, Melissa. The guy is sometimes scary. Maybe that's why I dreamt of him like he's some sort of villain. Dreams can be pretty silly, you know."

"Why is he scary to you?"

"Well, he has this strong male presence. He seems to be too much of a Martian to me."

"What do you mean by that?"

"You know, the men-are-from-Mars-women-are-from-Venus paradigm. I wonder what his zodiac sign is."

"Who knows, that may just be your impression, and behind that façade is a gentle person," Melissa reasoned out to her.

"Anyway, I don't think our paths will cross again. Yesterday's encounter was just a coincidence."

"Don't be too sure. Well, if you happen to bump into him again, it's meant to be."

Chapter

8

When she returned to work on Monday, Cara had forgotten Daniel Devereaux. There was much to do. To top it all, she was just beginning to feel her way within the organization and getting to know the people there. Her first month was, in fact, her familiarization period. Alec was pleased with her contribution at GCN. He learned from the *Pulse* people that Cara helped enhance the interview script. She poured herself into her work. There were press releases and communication reports to write which Alec assigned to her. The first half of the week was a whirl of deadlines. Later in the week, Alec reminded her that *Pulse* was airing the China episode at 10:00 p.m.

As she reached her apartment after work, Cara whipped up a meatless pasta dinner for herself. From work, she passed by the corner supermarket and bought the necessary ingredients. She cooked it with olive oil, threw in some sun-dried tomatoes, black olives, and sweet basil leaves. Then *voila*, she had a delicious dish. She believed her love for pasta must have something to do with the Italian in her. Cooking can be much fun in America with all the ingredients one needs readily available. After all, this is the land of plenty, she told herself.

She watched a couple of shows on TV after dinner, then she took a shower. After changing into her pajamas, she read two chapters from her book before it was time for *Pulse* to go on the air. Daniel Devereaux was a pleasure to watch, Cara admitted. He was not only telegenic, but his deep voice and interview savvy were more than come-ons for the show, and he asked the right questions. The interview dwelt on relevant issues in a well-organized format, easily sustaining viewer attention for a solid hour and thwarting any desire to change channels. She was glad she made a small contribution to the program script. The following morning, Cara dialed David Marsh's number from the calling card he gave her when they were introduced earlier.

"Hi, David. It's Cara. I just want to congratulate you for last night's program. It was very well done. Quite impressive. I have definitely something worthwhile to watch every night."

"Thank you, Cara. It's good to hear from you. How are things with you?"

"Everything's fine. I've been very busy these past three days. A lot of releases and reports to prepare."

"Well, it's good to be busy. It means you're needed. Listen, why don't I take you out to dinner? Are you free tomorrow night?"

"Tomorrow night is fine."

"Okay. I'll call you tomorrow morning at your office to confirm and get your address."

After their phone conversation, Cara wondered why she called David to congratulate him and not Daniel.

Well, he is the executive producer of the show, she justified to herself.

* * *

Cara left the office promptly after work to give herself time to get ready for her dinner date with David. He called her in the morning to confirm and to ask her if she liked Thai food. She happened to love Thai food. After work hours at GCN, Daniel sauntered into David's room.

"Feel like joining the guys for happy hour?," he asked David.

"I can't. I'm taking Cara out to dinner."

"Yeah? How is she?"

"She's fine. She says she has a lot of work, but she's not complaining. That's Cara."

"I happened to bump into her at the bookstore last weekend. Did you know she's a bookworm? I thanked her for helping us with the editing. Well, enjoy your dinner, and have a nice weekend."

"Thanks. You, too, Daniel."

* * *

David was punctual and was at Cara's door at the stroke of seven. Cara was wearing a midi printed dress with tiny floral designs, having abbreviated sleeves and a wide neckline, giving her a feminine look. David whistled in admiration when he saw her. David was of medium height and good-looking in a certain way with his shortly cropped dark brown hair and clean-cut appearance.

The restaurant was within walking distance. Thai restaurants were proliferating in the city and Thai food seemed to agree with New Yorkers' palates. After a satisfying meal, they lingered over their coffee with so much to talk about. They exchanged pleasantries and laughed heartily over them.

"You know, Cara, you do have an infectious sense of humor."

"I happen to come from a family that loves to joke and laugh."

"When you smile, your eyes smile, too. It becomes you, so you should really smile often."

"The people in my country smile a lot. It's the first thing tourists and visitors notice about us." She took a sip of her coffee. "David, may I ask you a question?"

"Sure."

"Why doesn't Daniel smile? I haven't seen him smile the whole time I was at GCN."

"He does smile, but I guess rarely. That has something to do with his parents' separation. They parted ways when they were already in their fifties. I remember he was terribly upset when it happened while we were completing our post-graduate studies. He hasn't been the same since. He's the only child. It's strange though that both parents aren't looking for other partners, but are now living apart in Long Island. Like a dutiful son, he visits each of them regularly on weekends."

"That's sad."

"Yeah. One columnist even described him as 'somber'. That's not an apt description of Daniel. Most often he's just in a pensive mood."

They decided to take a leisurely walk back to her apartment. The stars were out and the air was pleasantly cool. What Cara liked about Manhattan was that she felt safe, and her destinations were usually within walking distance.

"I had a nice time, David. Thank you."

"I enjoyed the evening, too, Cara. Let's keep in touch, okay?"

"I'd like that."

Chapter

9

It was a glorious Saturday morning. Cara decided to resume her running routine in Central Park. It was her form of exercise back home. She donned navy blue leggings emphasizing the shape of her legs and thighs, an aqua sleeveless tank top, and matching sneakers. She tied her hair in a ponytail. Since her arrival in New York, she had not exercised. Her face got a whiff of the morning air as she emerged from her apartment building. She loved that feeling. The flowers in the plant boxes lining the sidewalks were lovely even in their final glory at the close of summer, and competing with each other in a profusion of colors. Beautiful. She was a nature lover, and such sights never failed to brighten her mood.

Central Park was a jogger's paradise on bright mornings when the weather was agreeable. There were men and women jogging or walking, separately or in pairs. She spotted an entire family of five jogging together, including their small children. Cara watched them with amusement. She maintained her pace while following a circular path in the park. She decided to say her daily prayers while running. After completing five laps, she felt a little exhausted, so she reduced her speed, then plopped herself on the grass to rest and drink from her canteen.

"Giving up already?," said a familiar male voice. She turned to see Daniel in a T-shirt and jogging shorts. Nice masculine legs, Cara noted.

"I need to rest. I haven't exercised for some time," she answered in between breaths.

"You rest and I'll be back," he told her. It sounded more like a command.

After some time, Daniel returned and joined her on the grass.

"Are you all right?," he asked, seemingly concerned. "I guess so. I've rested a bit. I should really do this gradually from now on."

"Right. Do you want me to take you home?"

"Thank you, but it's not really necessary. I can walk."

"I'm walking home myself. C'mon, I don't want you fainting in the street."

They walked side by side. Cara could not help feeling conscious of this tall attractive man walking beside her. He kept glancing at her to check on her physical stability.

"Does your girlfriend run, too?," Cara asked Daniel.

"What girlfriend?"

"That attractive blonde from your office?"

"Oh, you mean Madeline. She's not my girlfriend." Cara could not explain why she felt relieved to hear this from him.

"This is where I live. Thank you for walking me home," she told him as they reached her apartment building.

"Remember to do it gradually next time. Take care now."

* * *

Cara spent the rest of Saturday indoors reading and occasionally turning on the TV. After a good night's sleep and breakfast, she attended the mid-morning Sunday Mass at St. Patrick's Cathedral. Right after the Mass, she entered Barnes & Noble to get her mother a birthday card. There was just a small number of people in the bookstore. She found the appropriate card and lingered along the aisles reading book titles. Turning to the next aisle, Cara could not believe her eyes. Daniel was standing there engrossed in a book. She sidled up to him quietly.

"We should stop meeting like this," she whispered to him. It caught him unaware and he responded with a pleased expression.

"Oh, hello, Cara. How are you feeling today?"

"Fine, thank you. You seem to have found another absorbing book."

"As a matter of fact, I have. It's a new one on media strategies. Are you in search for a particular title?"

"No. I just came out from Mass at St. Patrick's and decided to get my mother a card."

"I didn't see you there. I attended the previous Mass, too."

"You're Catholic?," she asked in a surprised tone. Cara sort of expected him to be maybe Jewish as many New Yorkers are.

"Yes. I guess I'm more of an on-and-off Catholic, but I attend Sunday Mass. Where did you sit?"

"On the left side in one of the middle pews."

"No wonder I didn't see you. I was on the opposite side towards the back. From here, I'm going to have coffee. Would you like to join me?"

"Okay."

They walked to the closest Starbucks outlet. After getting their coffee, Cara noted that Daniel used two servings of cream and a serving of sugar, just like her. They settled in a booth and sat facing each other. She had the chance to study his face at close range, and she realized how good-looking he really was. He had a well-chiseled masculine face, a defined jaw, thick eyebrows, and full lips. His best assets were his lush brown hair and expressive green eyes. Very attractive, she judged him silently. She took note of his big hands and clean fingernails, which were devoid of nail polish. She disliked nail polish in men, even the natural shade worn by some of them.

"Are you a coffee drinker?," he asked her while stirring his coffee.

"Yes, I am. I can't live without my morning cup. Don't you just love the smell of coffee brewing?"

"Somebody should invent coffee-scented perfume for coffee lovers." Cara found this amusing. He made the suggestion without smiling, but she knew he said it in jest.

Music suddenly floated in with Frank Sinatra singing "*They Can't Take That Away From Me*".

"Ah, Sinatra. I like that song." Cara commented and hummed with the music.

"You like Sinatra?"

"He's one of my favorite singers. I developed a liking for him since I was just a little girl…influenced by my parents I suppose since his tapes were constantly being played at home." Daniel stared at her in disbelief. She likes books and coffee, she runs for exercise like him, and now Sinatra. These are my interests, he thought. Too much of a coincidence.

"I guess I'm kinda old-fashioned in my taste in music. I go for old favorites and classical."

"Same thing here." Daniel replied. "I don't like anything loud, so I don't really enjoy discos much. But I also appreciate the music of the Earth, Wind and Fire, and the Commodores."

"Me, too. *Reasons, Miracles,* and *September*? *Machine Gun*?

"Right." Daniel was even more amazed. "Tell me more about yourself, Cara."

"What do you want to know?"

"Well, what is your passion, your other interests, and beliefs perhaps?"

"I'm basically a simple person with simple tastes. I love books, of course. I like going to the movies and solving crossword puzzles. I go to work early and I start my day solving the daily crossword puzzle. I'm pro-life and I'm an environmentalist. I enjoy the arts – theaters, museums, and exhibits. I like Shakespeare's sonnets. Sonnet 116 is my favorite. I don't favor divorce, premarital sex, live-in arrangements, same-sex marriages, and capital punishment, not necessarily in that order. That's quite a mouthful. You must think I'm old-fashioned and boring," she said, giving him a look of uncertainty while anticipating his reaction.

"On the contrary, I didn't think your kind still exists. You know, with the permissiveness of the times and in the advent of new technologies, you're an endangered species. I like movies myself. What type of movies do you watch?"

"All sorts really. I like period movies. I also go for comedy and romance. I even watch adventure movies like *Indiana Jones, Superman, Batman, Zorro,* and *Star Wars.*"

"Really? I enjoy those, too. So, what are your goals and priorities in life?"

"I want to give my best to whatever I do, to be of service to others, and to author a book during my lifetime. I want to work with poor children. I also hope to get married someday and raise a family. I want to fall head over heels first. As Anthony Hopkins said in the movie *Meet Joe Black*, "you should be swept away, levitate, sing with rapture and dance like a dervish because there's no sense living your life if you're not deeply in love.' I want that. Of course, I want to marry my soul mate, although I've yet to meet him," she said wistfully. "Well, as they say, lightning could strike."

"Marriage must be far from your mind right now. You seem quite young."

"I'm not as young as you think. I'm 25 years old," she said smiling. "Most Asians just look younger than their actual age. I'm one of them."

"Wow, you don't look a day older than 20," he declared, giving her an I-don't- believe-it look. "You didn't mention about success or money." He observed her intently.

"I guess personal fulfillment is more important to me, and it may not even have anything to do with money or success. If you're fulfilled, you're in a way successful, don't you think?" He nodded in agreement. "Now your turn," she said nudgingly.

"Well, I love sports. I play tennis. I played basketball in high school and in college. I enjoy swimming. I also ski during winter. Aside from running, I go to the gym to keep fit. I didn't imagine being on television and becoming an anchor. My first job was as an apprentice at NBC. I moved to GCN and became a producer. I got the anchor's seat when David and I conceptualized *Pulse*. I mean, I wasn't really aiming for it, but it was handed to me."

"You deserve it. GCN was bound to see your talent sooner or later. Are you a workaholic?"

"No. I work hard within limits, but I'm not a workaholic."

"Have you heard of Workaholics Anonymous? They held a convention and nobody came because everybody was working."

It made Daniel laugh. Cara liked his laugh, and it surprised her that he could laugh like that.

"What do you believe in?," she asked him.

"I do believe in saving the environment, I'm also pro-life, and I don't agree with same-sex marriages. I believe in marriage even if my parents are separated. I'm basically conservative. Do you like sports?"

"Yes. I used to play tennis, but I've neglected the game. I like baseball and basketball as a spectator. I was in my school's track and field team."

"What teams do you root for?"

"The Knicks and the Yankees, of course, but when Michael Jordan was playing, I cheered for the Bulls. I admire the guy. Are you the adventurous type?"

"Well, I've done a lot of crazy and daring things in my twenties like sky diving, scuba diving, and going down high ski slopes. You can say I've somewhat mellowed. I haven't scaled mountains yet and I don't intend to. I don't think I'd like to try bungee jumping either. How about you, are you adventurous?"

"Not really. I joined my friends once mountain climbing, but they were actually just hills by normal standards. There was a waterfall near the top and we had a picnic up there. It was nice and cool with a panoramic view of the city. I've also gone river rafting. It was quite exciting."

"You know, Cara, I believe we can be good friends. We practically have the same interests. Not even David shares most of my interests, and he's my closest friend."

"Here's to friendship," Cara said, raising her coffee cup to his.

Two youngish women in the next table apparently recognized Daniel. They approached and asked him for his autograph. The price of popularity, Cara thought.

"Doesn't it bother you? You know, autograph seekers," she asked him.

"I value my privacy, but I guess it's a small price to pay for being on television."

"Be consoled you're not a movie star. It could be worse."

"I can imagine. Are you going to work in New York permanently, may I ask?"

"No, I'm here on a one-year renewable contract with the U.N. I used to work with a business conglomerate back home. I've always wanted to work with a nonprofit organization for a change. This job at UNDP is my window of opportunity. I like New York and I have friends and relatives here."

"So, do you have a boyfriend back home?" It caught her by surprise because she did not expect such a personal question from him.

"No."

"A pretty woman like you? You must be choosy."

"I had a boyfriend of long standing, but we broke up when he left for the U.S. for further medical studies. I haven't heard from him since. It's been years, and he must be married by now. I believe one should really choose well because in this day and age, nothing seems to be permanent anymore."

"You're right there." After a slight pause, he said, "Since you seem to like music, you may want to join us at GCN. We usual ly have this *karaoke* sing-along session on Fridays at the office lounge. It's our way of unwinding after a week of working. You'd be surprised how many frustrated singers there are at GCN. You'll hear a lot of budding Sinatras."

"Including you?"

"Including me," he answered with a smile. He did have a nice smile, Cara observed, and he had a perfect set of teeth. You should really smile more often, Daniel, she wanted to tell him.

"I may just take you up on that."

Chapter

10

Cara was beginning to like Daniel. Her initial negative perception of him vanished after finding him likable, and discovering they enjoyed the same things. So he thought she was pretty. Cara felt like confiding to someone. It was Georgia whom she could trust. Georgia was already at her desk one early morning at work.

"Good morning, Georgia. Do you have time to talk?"

"Hi, Cara. You picked the right time. Alec has a morning meeting and won't be back till noon. What's up? It sounds serious, my dear. Let's go to your cubicle."

They settled themselves in Cara's cubicle where they had some privacy.

"Georgia, I just want to share something with you. I've been bumping into Daniel Devereaux often this past week, at the bookstore twice, and while running in Central Park. Yesterday he asked me to join him for coffee and we had a pleasant talk. We discovered we have a lot in common. He seems nice."

"Really? I'm glad to hear that." Georgia replied with obvious excitement.

"I'm a bit concerned because of his reputation as a playboy. He told me he wants us to be friends."

"That's good, Cara. You should get to know him better."

"I'm confused, Georgia. Now that I'm beginning to know him, I seem to enjoy his company."

"There's nothing wrong with that. Just be careful, my dear. I don't want to see you hurt. He's a celebrity, you know, and a lot of women are interested in him. Beware of Madeline Foster. She thinks Daniel Devereaux is her property. Get to know him as a person. There must be more to him than just his good looks."

"Thanks, Georgia. Please keep this to yourself. I just needed to talk to someone I can trust."

"Anytime you want to talk, I'm here. I must admit this is getting to be quite exciting," Georgia said gleefully.

* * *

Cara had Filipino friends in New York. Josie and Cristy both worked at the U.N., and Trisha was with the Ford Foundation, just across the U.N. They made plans to go out for dinner and agreed to meet at the U.N. Hotel lobby. Trisha suggested they go to an exotic restaurant in Manhattan east. It was a quaint place which offered some privacy. It was just the right venue for them to talk and share about what was going on in their respective lives. They picked a side table a few paces from the entrance. As they got seated, Trisha looked around the restaurant, which was only half-filled that early evening.

"There's Daniel Devereaux," Trisha told them, pleased with seeing someone important. Cara turned to look and met Daniel's eyes. He waved at her and she waved back. He was with a young woman in a business suit. Her friends turned to her simultaneously with a questioning look.

"You know Daniel Devereaux?," Trisha asked in wonderment.

"I worked with him and his staff briefly on the script for the Secretary-General's interview on *Pulse*."

"He remembers you," Josie commented. "Is he nice?"

"Oh, yes."

"Hey, he's headed this way," Cristy warned them.

"Hi, Cara, fancy seeing you here," Daniel said as he stopped at their table.

"Hi, Daniel. We seem to bump into each other in unlikely places. I want you to meet my friends." Cara introduced each of them to him and he shook their hands.

"I'm meeting with the health care representative on my parents' behalf." He looked at each of Cara's friends. "It's nice meeting you." Then he turned to Cara. "I'll be seeing you," he told her before returning to his table.

"Cara, why was he explaining to you?," Trisha wanted to know.

"I don't know."

"It looks like business because there are papers in front of them," Josie said. "He's even more good-looking in person."

"Did you notice his eyes? They're green," Trisha took note. "You don't seem to be mere acquaintance, Cara, the way he sounded."

"Well, we're friends."

Cara tried to hold back her tongue. She could not admit to them that she was attracted to Daniel Devereaux. Not yet.

* * *

Cara plunged herself into her work, hoping to keep Daniel out of her mind, but getting home after work was another story. He kept intruding into her thoughts. She remembered Georgia's words and vowed to be careful. Her week passed uneventfully, and then it was Friday. She arrived at work early as usual and sat down at her desk to tackle the day's crossword puzzle while sipping her morning coffee. She was close to solving the entire puzzle when her phone rang.

"Good morning, Cara. It's Daniel. Are you done with your puzzle?"

"Hi, Daniel. Almost solved. What can I do for you?"

"Would you like to join us for *karaoke* tonight after work? It starts at 6:00 at the GCN lounge."

"That may be a good idea. I'll try to be there. I want to hear you guys sing."

"Good. So, how was your week?"

"Pretty hectic, but manageable."

"You're doing all right." After a brief pause, he said, "We hope to see you tonight. Bye, Cara." He said 'we' and not 'I', Cara noted.

* * *

David met Cara as she entered the GCN lounge. Daniel, who was across the room, waved at her. He was with Madeline. Cara joined David, Josh, Victor, and a couple of *Pulse* producers. They offered her a drink, and she accepted a Coke. Attention was riveted on the guy singing *It's Impossible*. After finishing his song, he received a rowdy vote of approval from his officemates. A lady was next, and she belted out *New York, New York* with gusto, to the delight of the audience.

"She's one of our secretaries," David told Cara.

"She has a terrific voice. It looks like she's in the wrong profession," Cara commented.

"Let's ask Daniel to sing," David suggested. They started to chant his name, and the others in the room followed. Daniel took the microphone. He rolled up the sleeves of his white shirt.

"You're going to pay for this, guys," he remarked.

He started to sing *I Thought About You*, popularized by Frank Sinatra, with a bouncy beat. The guys pretended to swoon, while the women swayed with the tempo. Cara detected a trace of Sinatra in his voice, although he could hold his own. He had talent and style. At the end of his number, there was a clamor for an encore, but Daniel replied "That's it, guys."

"If none of you is going to sing yet, I'm going to the ladies room," Cara said.

"Second door to your left," Josh directed her.

Cara powdered her face and dabbed on some lipstick. The door opened and Madeline entered. She stood next to Cara and glared menacingly at her through the mirror. Cara ignored her.

"Stay away from Daniel if you know what's good for you," Madeline warned her.

"Excuse me?," Cara replied looking at her through the mirror.

"You heard me. Don't play coy with me, woman. I know you're after Daniel," she said in an acerbic tone.

"What are you saying? What, may I ask, gave you that impression?" Cara maintained her composure.

"You have your own brand of flirting, and I've seen Daniel's reaction. Well, for your information, he's already taken."

"For your information, I'm not flirting with him and I have no designs on him." Cara continued to keep her cool without raising her voice.

"You should know you're not good enough for him. You belong to an inferior race. A man like Daniel deserves someone better."

"You mean, someone like you? You know, you just proved yourself inferior with your condescending attitude." Cara stormed out of the room and collided with David.

"Cara, what's wrong?" He took her hand and led her to a corner.

"It's Madeline. She said terrible things to me."

She could not stop the tears from flowing. David immediately took her in his arms. She rested her head on his shoulder and took comfort in his embrace. She related to David that Madeline accused her of flirting with Daniel, and she belittled her and her race. The belittling part hurt Cara the most.

Daniel, who was on his way to the men's room, spied them in this position, and frowned. After Cara simmered down, David told her to wait in the building lobby so he could take her home while he got his coat. On his way out of the men's room, Daniel encountered David leaving.

"I'm taking Cara home. Something happened which agitated her. I'll be back and I'll tell you all about it." David told Daniel.

"Is she all right?"

"She was crying, but she's all right now."

When David returned, he proceeded directly to his office and dialed Daniel's cellphone. He asked him to meet him there where he related to Daniel what Cara revealed to him.

"I should talk to Madeline. This is going too far. So, is there anything between you and Cara? I saw you two embracing."

"No, Daniel. I was just comforting her. I'm already committed to Isabel. She will be returning soon from Colombia, and I plan to ask her to marry me. You seem relieved. Are you interested in Cara? She's a gem of a woman, Daniel."

"I know. We have common interests, and I enjoy her company."

* * *

"Good morning, handsome," Madeline said in greeting, sashaying into Daniel's office seductively. The room was enveloped by a cloud of her pungent perfume.

"Hello, Madeline. You're just the person I want to talk to. Sit down."

"What's up? Are you going to make my day, huh?" She sat down, put her elbows on Daniel's desk and leaned towards him, a flirtatious smile plastered on her face.

"It's about what you said to Cara. That wasn't very nice." Madeline's smile faded abruptly and she straightened up in her chair.

"That Asian woman? Did she tell on me?," she reacted with controlled fury.

"No, she did not, but David made her relate the incident to him. She was hurt."

"What's it to you, Daniel? Why should you care anyway?," she questioned him.

"Because I like Cara," he said without hesitation, catching Madeleine by surprise.

"You don't really mean that, do you?"

"Yes, I do. In fact, I'm concerned because she was my guest last Friday."

Madeline was jolted. She rose and went to his side. "But what about us, Daniel? Are you forgetting what we have?"

"There's no 'us', Madeline. You know that." He then stood up to distance himself from her and subtly walked a few paces away.

"You can't be serious. Not her, Daniel," she said in a more subdued tone. "She's not like us. She's different." She was making a futile attempt to open his eyes.

"Cara is a human being just like us. She's intelligent and she's a fine specimen of womanhood," he answered her firmly, facing her squarely.

"Don't be a fool, Daniel. You're making a big mistake," she said, pointing her index finger at him, and left his office in a huff. Daniel heaved a sigh of relief.

Chapter

11

Cara deferred going to the bookstore and put off running in Central Park for a while. She did not want to run into Daniel. The situation was already awkward as it was, and she did not want to cause him further trouble. If she kept her distance, maybe he would realize that she was not out to entrap him. Suppose he thought that those times that they bumped into each other were pre-planned by her? She shuddered at the thought. She decided not to take any calls in the meantime, so when her phone in the office or at the apartment rang, she waited for the answering machine to take it, and she listened first to see who the caller was. David called just to say hello and to ask how she was. Melissa wanted to know why she did not pick up the phone right away, but she could not tell her yet. There were a couple of calls where the person on the other line did not utter a word. She wondered who would be calling her without leaving any message.

That weekend the faucet in her sink would not close well and dripped continuously. The building super promised to send the handyman to look at it. Cara was in shorts and reading her new book in her living room when the doorbell rang. Thank God the handyman is here, she said to herself. She opened the door, and there was Daniel standing outside. Cara stared at him long with surprise written on her face.

"Aren't you going to ask me in?," he said

"I'm sorry. I was expecting the handyman. Please come in."

"One of the tenants in your building let me in. I guess I didn't look questionable to him. Nice place you have here," he said, making a sweeping survey. "I haven't seen you for some time, and I'm just wondering how you are. Are you all right?"

"I'm fine." She led him to the living room where they sat down.

"You haven't been running. I tried to call you but I didn't want to talk to a machine that can't reply to me, so I decided to see you personally." So it was he who called, Cara figured out.

"David told me what happened. I'm sorry with what Madeline put you through. I talked to her and it's over between us. There was really nothing to begin with. We just dated occasionally. So, are we still friends?"

"I guess so. I'm sorry if Madeline's racist language affected me. Racial overtones always do, and I'm very sensitive about these things. I often cry for African-Americans every time I watch something on TV which berates them because of the color of their skin. It's inhuman. We were all created equal, you know."

"I agree with you," he answered, nodding his head slightly.

"When I was pursuing my studies here, I felt it, too. They regard people of other races differently. My close friend and confidante at UNDP happens to be

African-American. The U.N. must be the only place where I don't feel any racial discrimination, and I'm glad I'm working there."

"I understand, Cara. I'm anti-racist myself," he assured her.

"Tell me honestly, Daniel. Do you believe I'm flirting with you?"

"No," he replied readily, although he was taken aback by her frankness.

"That's settled then. Madeline accused me of flirting with you."

"Forget Madeline. Actually, I don't see anything wrong if you flirt with me, Cara," he said with a soft expression on his face, and she felt uneasy.

"Let's change the subject. May I offer you something to drink?"

"No, thank you. I'm on my way to Long Island to visit my parents." He stood up. Cara took the cue and moved with him slowly towards the door.

"By the way, you sing well."

"Thank you, Cara." He was pleased with her compliment. "So, I'll be seeing you?"

She nodded her head and went to the door to open it for him, her back facing him.

"You've got great legs," he commented.

"Daniel, you're embarrassing me."

"Can't I compliment a friend? I just happen to be a legs man." He gave her his rare smile. "Take care of yourself."

"Thanks for dropping by."

She was simply elated that Daniel took the time to check how she was. She played a tape of Frank Sinatra, swinging to the beat of the music and dancing with an imaginary partner. She was happy at the prospect of seeing him again.

Chapter

12

"Alec is in the hospital," Georgia told Cara as she barged into her cubicle one morning. "His wife Diane called. Apparently he had palpitations yesterday. She said it's nothing serious, but his doctor advised confinement until his tests are complete. Diane didn't sound worried, so I guess he's okay."

"Where is he confined?"

"At Mount Sinai Hospital. I asked Diane if he's allowed to receive visitors, and she said it's all right. In fact, she thinks it might cheer him up. I'm ordering flowers to be delivered to the hospital. Why don't we visit him after work?"

"Good idea. Count me in."

* * *

Alec was sitting up in bed when Georgia, Cara, and Valerie arrived at the hospital. Wife Diane was attending to him. He did not look sick and his cheeks had a pinkish tint.

"You look well, Alec," Georgia complimented him.

"I should be able to leave the hospital tomorrow. My doctor did some tests and is monitoring my condition, and the palpitations haven't recurred since. I have a good doctor and I have faith in him."

Just then Alec's doctor entered the room with a nurse. He was a tall, dark, and attractive man in white. Cara stared at him wide-eyed.

"Joey? Is that you?," Cara exclaimed. She could not believe it was her ex-boyfriend she was seeing.

"Cara! What are you doing here?" He approached her and wrapped his arms around her, while the others in the room watched with growing curiosity.

"I'm working at the U.N., and Alec happens to be my boss."

"I can't believe it's you after all these years." He turned to Alec and the rest with his arm draped over Cara's shoulder. "Cara was my girlfriend back home."

"Oh," they responded in unison.

"The last news I received about you was that you were at Johns Hopkins Hospital in Baltimore," Cara told Joey, while the rest listened.

"I was. I moved here two years ago. How are you?"

"I'm fine. I'm enjoying my work here."

"I'm glad to hear that."

Alec introduced him. "I want you all to meet Dr. Jose Castelo, Jr., my doctor."

After shaking their hands, Joey approached Alec's bed. "I've good news for you, Mr. Stevenson. There's nothing seriously wrong with you. Your test results came out negative. I have prepared your discharge slip. If you feel anything unusual, just give me a call. In the meantime, I'm giving you a suggested diet to bring down your bad cholesterol level. Your blood test shows it's slightly elevated, but nothing to be alarmed about."

"Thank you, doctor. That's a relief. When can I return to work?"

"You may go back to work anytime you feel like it, Mr. Stevenson. You're the best judge."

Before leaving, Joey asked Cara privately to stay behind so they could talk. She told Georgia about it.

"Your ex-boyfriend is handsome and nice, Cara. How do you feel seeing him again?"

"Surprised. I didn't expect to see him here." Cara was still giddy with surprise.

Joey led Cara to his office at the hospital. He seemed to be doing very well in his medical practice. He was not yet married. He claimed he had no time to settle down with the demands of his profession.

"I haven't forgotten you, babe." 'Babe' was his pet name for Cara. "I haven't been involved with anybody since then. I seemed to have lost touch with everybody back home, even Vincent. I've really been very busy, and my patients are my priority right now. You can't imagine how many people have heart ailments, and most of them are men. I'm now performing heart surgery." He took Cara's hand in his and gazed into her eyes. "You're even more beautiful now than I can remember, babe. You're not married, are you?"

"Why, do I look married to you?," Cara threw back his question, smiling.

"No, but you do look happy. There must be someone special in your life who's responsible for this obvious glow in you. You look radiant."

"There's really nothing I can tell you at the moment, Joey, but there's someone I have feelings for."

"Lucky guy. I'd like to meet him. Do you think he'll mind if I take you out to dinner? I'm knocking off in a few minutes."

"It's okay."

He took her to a cozy Italian restaurant in Manhattan. They talked about a variety of topics, about their common friends and their respective families, mostly catching up on lost time. Cara's brother Vince, who was also a surgeon, and Joey were best friends.

"Where's Vince practicing orthopedics?"

"He's at St. John's Hospital in Chicago. You know, he doesn't even know I'm here in the U.S. because it was a quick decision on my part to come here. I meant to call or e-mail him at least, but I got busy and I forgot altogether."

"Give him my regards when you communicate with him, will you?"

"I'll do that."

He dropped her off at her apartment building.

"I miss you, babe, and I want to see you again. Okay with you?"

"Of course, Joey," she assured him.

"Let's get together some time. Take in a movie perhaps and dinner? We have some reconnection to make. It's been a long time."

"Fine with me."

"I'll call you. Good night, babe." He gave her a hug and a kiss on the cheek.

* * *

Cara and Joey had known each other since they were children. They were next-door neighbors in the same upper middle-class subdivision. It did not start well between them when they were small because Joey was full of mischief when he was a boy. When Cara was just a girl, she watched a basketball game at the gym within their subdivision with her friends. Joey and his gang sat behind them and he stuck a bubble gum in Cara's hair. Her mom had to snip off that portion of her hair, and Cara hated Joey for that. He made her cry. When Joey's mom found out about it, she urged him to apologize to Cara. Joey went to Cara's house to apologize. He sounded very sincere, so Cara relented, and from then on, they became friends. Joey and Vince were of the same age, five years older than Cara. They were classmates at the Ateneo de Manila, the country's foremost school for boys, from grade school through high school, then at the State University for their Medical course, so Joey was a regular at the Marino home.

Even when they were still small, both Vince and Joey already showed an inclination towards becoming doctors early on. Once when Cara played with her favorite doll, they borrowed it from her, insisting that her doll was sick. Then they pretended to administer medicine to Cara's doll and swathed it in bandages. They even executed a *post mortem* on one of her old dolls and gave it a decent burial by digging a hole in the yard and burying it, complete with a funeral march they composed.

Cara was not an avid participant in boy activities because she found them too rough for her taste. She had a *yaya* (nanny) as an infant then as a toddler, like in most Filipino families. When she was of school age, she was brought to school by the family driver and accompanied by her *yaya*. It was only when she turned 18 that she was allowed to drive one of their cars, but rarely alone. She was usually with Melissa because they went to the same university in their college years. A major part of her girlhood was spent with her mother. She was her mother's alter ego and constant companion. When she blossomed into a lady, her mother became her confidante. Vince was not imposed the same restrictions as Cara, simply because he was male. Although his activities were closely monitored by their parents, he had expanded freedom in his social life. He could go out on dates without much scrutiny.

Joey turned out to be a responsible adult. He followed his father's footsteps and became a heart doctor. He and Cara were a twosome. Their respective parents were hoping that they would eventually get married since they were already familiar with each other's family backgrounds. Filipino parents are often concerned with their children's choices, and prefer that they marry someone from a family they already know. Cara and Joey became sweethearts until he left for the U.S., and only then did they agree to break off their relationship. Joey's family moved to a suburban neighborhood, and Cara lost touch of them. She had a string of suitors, including a couple of persistent ones offering marriage, but she did not want to enter into another relationship after Joey, and instead concentrated on her career.

When she was already working in this big corporation back home, none of the guys courting her even made her heart miss a beat. She was not keen on getting involved with anyone romantically, and there were many. Cara was a head-turner. Filipinos normally have the bad habit of staring, and she hated it when men stared at her. She was not classified as *suplada* or snobbish since she had a smile for everybody, but deep down inside her she was annoyed with male attention. This could be one of the reasons she wanted to get far away from her home city. Her friends defined her mien as faithfulness to Joey. Cara only felt she was not ready to replace Joey.

The most compelling reason for Cara's departure from her country was her disgust with the government. The president who was elected into office by popular vote of the *masa* or general public was an uneducated former movie star who did not know a thing or two about running the country. He was a gambler, an alcoholic, and a womanizer, the latter he flaunted. His open display of immorality and maintaining several mistresses were repugnant to most Filipinos. In his first months in office, there was already widespread corruption. Crime was up, particularly kidnapping of wealthy Chinese. His personal friends were favored with juicy contracts and top positions. He himself and his different families were wallowing in luxury, which a president's salary could never justify. The company Cara worked for was not spared of politics. The value of the peso was plummeting pitifully, and the people were dissatisfied with the sagging economy. Cara told her parents that she was not escaping, but only needed a change of scenery.

Chapter

13

Autumn in New York was in full regalia. Drizzles were already a constant visitor, and New Yorkers had to be armed with umbrellas when venturing out or risk getting wet, and most likely catch the flu. The beauty of autumn is never more evident than in the trees when their foliage become daringly orange before welcoming winter. Sort of a last hurrah for them. Being incurably romantic, autumn descended on Cara as a melancholic season. All these, and the cold beginning its assault, ushered in a wave of nostalgia. She missed her parents and her brother. They emailed each other regularly, but she decided to call her parents, and she felt better after their conversation.

* * *

On a partly sunny Saturday morning, Cara decided to run again. Exercise was not her only reason. She wanted to catch a glimpse of Daniel. Sure enough, Daniel came running towards her. He turned around and changed direction to join her.

"Good morning, Cara. I'm glad you're back on track."

"Hi, Daniel."

They continued to run with Daniel in the lead. Sometimes they ran abreast and he would turn his head towards her as if to check how she was holding up. After several uninterrupted laps, Cara told him she was quitting.

She found a free bench and sat down, and he sat beside her.

"I'm through myself. I've already done a few rounds before you came," he said.

They did some cooling-down exercises for a few minutes then sat down again.

"You know what? I had the surprise of my life. Alec was confined at Mount Sinai Hospital recently for palpitations and we visited him there. You know who his doctor is? My former boyfriend Joey. I told you about him. I couldn't believe he's just here in New York all this time, and still single."

"Maybe he's still carrying the torch for you." Daniel was probing.

"I don't think so. We had dinner and just talked for old time's sake. He said he hasn't forgotten me, but it's really over between us."

"You're sure?"

"Yes." Cara wondered why it mattered to him. Maybe he just wanted to make conversation.

"By the way, I recall you mentioned that you want to work with poor children. There's this place on 8th Avenue which provides shelter for abandoned children. Would you like to go there?," he asked her.

"I'd love to," she replied enthusiastically.

"Are you free tomorrow morning? I can pick you up."

"Aren't you going to visit your parents?"

"I have time for that in the afternoon. I'll pick you up at 9:00."

* * *

Daniel wore a casual jacket, which gave him that jaunty look. Cara brought a handful of children's books and a big bag of cookies she bought the day before.

Cara was not prepared for what she saw. The children were of different ages, ranging from a few months to about 10 years old, predominantly black with a few Latinos and whites. She told Daniel that she could not understand why parents would just abandon their children. It was downright cruel. Her heart cried out to them. The children remained in the shelter until they were adopted, and sometimes it was a long wait.

Daniel accepted a three-month-old baby from one of the caregivers, who taught him how to carry the infant properly. The caregiver explained to them that babies needed warmth from a human body, so they had to be carried sometimes. Cara took a peek at the baby in Daniel's arms. The baby, a black boy, was smiling at Daniel with his big eyes fixed on him. Seeing Daniel like this with the children made Cara appreciate him more. This was definitely a nonplayboy image of him.

"You're a natural," Cara told him. "Why, he likes you. He's adorable. Look at those long eyelashes." Cara kissed the baby's forehead.

Cara read *Peter Pan* to the older kids and they were all ears. One five-year-old black girl was particularly talkative. Her name was Paisley, and she followed Cara around.

"Am I ugly?," the child asked Cara.

"No, Paisley, of course not."

"Our neighbor in Brooklyn said I'm ugly."

"Remember this, Paisley, nobody is ugly in the eyes of God. You're a pretty little girl and you're special," she assured her in front of Daniel.

As they were about to leave, Paisley tugged at Cara's skirt.

"Are you coming back?"

"Yes, I'm coming back. I'll read to you another story next time. Okay? Now give me a big hug." Paisley hugged Cara tightly.

Cara hugged the children, and Daniel followed suit.

Inside Daniel's vehicle, Cara covered her face with her hands.

"Cara, is something wrong?"

"I'm okay. I'm just overwhelmed. Those children are so pitiful and lonely. What future can they look forward to?"

Her eyes were brimming with tears. Daniel drew her to him with one arm around her and he let her head rest on his shoulder. She had never been this close to him and she experienced a warmth which soothed her.

"I'm just as affected as you are. Most of those children were abandoned because of poverty, and this is supposed to be rich America."

"I appreciate your taking me there, Daniel." She felt his lips on her hair.

Chapter

14

Cara was shopping for casual thick clothing at the GAP store in Manhattan. After making her purchase, she moved towards the exit. Suddenly someone bumped her accidentally, and she turned to look.

"I'm sorry. I wasn't looking," said a young white woman with a peculiar accent.

"It's all right," Cara answered. They stared at each other briefly.

There was something familiar about her and her foreign accent. Do I know her?, Cara asked herself. There was a flicker of recognition in the eyes of the woman, but she did not say anything else and moved away. Cara walked out to the street, then at the spur of the moment decided to turn back. She convinced herself that if she really knew this woman, she might regret it if she did not even say hello. Cara searched the store, spotted her inspecting an item, and approached her.

"Hi, you look very familiar. Have we met before? I'm Cara Marino."

"Cara! It's really you. It's Inge, your classmate in high school, remember?"

"Inge! I didn't recognize you. You look different. You're slimmer and your hair is longer. It must be ten years since we last saw each other. What are you doing in New York?"

"I've been here for a year with my husband. He's on a two-year teaching contract with New York University."

"So you're married. How long have you been married?"

"Two years, but we have no children. How about you, Cara, why are you in New York?"

"I'm here temporarily. I'm also working on contract with the U.N. How nice to see you, Inge, after all these years. Let's go some place where we can talk."

They went to the nearest cafe. Inge came from Austria. Her father was former Austrian ambassador to the Philippines. They went to the same exclusive school for girls, Maryknoll College, and they became the best of friends. After their high school graduation, Inge's father was reassigned to another country, and that was the last they saw of each other.

"Cara, I'm very lonely here. I have no friends, and I'm not comfortable with New Yorkers."

"You have a friend now, Inge."

"You're heaven-sent, Cara. I've nobody to talk to, and sometimes I need to pour out my heart to someone."

"Is something bothering you? You can tell me. Remember how we used to tell each other our secrets?"

"It's my husband. I suspect he's having an affair."

"That's sad. I hope you're wrong, Inge. Is he Austrian?"

"Yes. He's also from Vienna. His name is Bernard. We've known each other for a long time, even before my father was assigned to the Philippines, so everybody expected us to marry. We had a good marriage at the start, but when we came here, he changed. He started coming home late and he gets phone calls from a woman. He says she's just one of his students seeking his advice. I trusted him and I wouldn't have suspected anything if he hadn't become less demonstrative towards me. I can feel it, Cara. I'm not working so I'm totally dependent on him. He's all I have here, and when he's not home, I go out to keep my mind off things."

"Did you articulate your feelings to him?"

"I tried, but he's evasive, and I don't want to quarrel."

"I'm not married, Inge, but I can give you some advice. I believe you should have a heart-to-heart talk with Bernard. Suppose he'll admit to having an affair, what do you plan to do?"

"I don't think I can accept it, Cara. I'll probably make plans to go home to Vienna. What's the use of staying with him if he's only fooling me."

"I see your point. I don't think I can tolerate infidelity either. When you decide to confront Bernard, just keep your cool. Don't get angry. Now that we've found each other, Inge, let's keep in touch. You can always talk to me. I'll give you my contact numbers."

"Thank you, Cara. I need your friendship more than ever now."

"I remember you used to write beautiful poetry. Do you still do that?"

"Yes, when the inspiration comes. I notice poetry flows easily when one is in an emotional upheaval."

"I loved your poems, Inge."

Their common love for poetry was one of the reasons which brought them closer together. They were both very romantic. They reminisced about their school days, their classmates, and the nuns. Their favorite nun was pretty Sister Rose Anthony, who was rumored to be a former

Miss New York. She was every student's friend because she had a sunny disposition. She would stop to converse with the students and inquire about their activities and their families.

Inge had pleasant memories about the Philippines, and she missed it. Her family had not been back there since.

"You know what I want to do right now, Inge? I want to go up the Empire State Building. I always do that when I'm in New York, and I haven't done it yet since I arrived."

"I'm with you," Inge said with matching enthusiasm.

"There's something romantic about the Empire State Building. I've watched *An Affair to Remember, Sleepless in Seattle,* and *Love Affair* several times, and I cried each time."

"You know, Cara, it has the same effect on me," Inge remarked with excitement.

They were glad that they felt the same. They walked to the Empire State Building and took the elevator up to the viewing deck. They stayed there for some time just looking down New York City.

"Just imagine Cary Grant and Warren Beatty waiting here patiently for hours, even enduring a thunderstorm," Cara said.

"Yes, and all for love. Tom Hanks and Meg Ryan also finally met each other right here," Inge added. "You know, the two of us are hopeless romantics." They laughed at themselves.

"Do you have a boyfriend, Cara?"

"Not right now. You remember Joey Castelo, don't you?"

"Yes, that cute neighbor of yours."

"He became my boyfriend in college. He's now a heart surgeon here in New York. We broke up when he left for the U.S. to specialize. Recently we bumped into each other accidentally, but I don't think we'll get back together again. I will always have feelings for him, but that's all. There's someone I have a crush on, Inge."

"Well, we're never too old for crushes."

"You've probably seen him on TV. Daniel Devereaux?"

"Of course, that gorgeous anchor. I watch his program. Do you know him?"

"I've spent time with him having coffee, running in Central Park, and visiting the abandoned children's center. We seem to like the same things, and I can't get him out of my mind."

"You'll know eventually if he's the right one for you, Cara."

* * *

The following week, Joey called Cara as he promised. He asked her if she wanted to see a movie that day and have dinner afterwards. He said it was one of those rare days when he could knock off at the hospital early. Cara agreed, and he picked her up at her office after work. She felt at ease in Joey's company, and he held her hand like old times.

"You know, I haven't seen a movie in ages," Joey confessed to her.

"That's not good, Joey. You need some form of recreation or you'll get stressed out. We used to watch a lot of movies before you became a doctor," she reminded him.

"I know. I play tennis occasionally on weekends with the other doctors at the hospital. That's about all the recreation I get, plus reading."

They had dinner after the movie. Unknown to Cara, Daniel was in the same restaurant waiting for a high school classmate. She was not in the habit of surveying her surroundings, particularly in public places, so she had no way of spotting him. Daniel saw them enter the restaurant. He was seated in the elevated section and was not visible to them, but he was able to observe them. His former classmate called to say that he would be slightly delayed, so Daniel's attention was riveted to the direction of Cara and her date for several minutes while waiting for his friend. He observed that she behaved in a relaxed manner in the company of her tall and good-looking date, who, he deduced must be her former boyfriend. He seemed Filipino in a way. Daniel was drawn to Cara's smile, and tonight she was smiling a lot and laughing at what her date was saying. The way she moved while expressing with her hands was femininely graceful. It was almost lyrical. She is beautiful, and I'm attracted to her, he was thinking to himself. The attraction became even more pronounced after discovering the kind of person she was. When his friend arrived, Daniel could only steal a glance at the pair. He noticed that when they left the restaurant, Cara's date had his arm around her shoulder in a possessive sort of way, and Daniel realized that it bothered him.

Chapter

15

A week before Thanksgiving, Daniel asked Cara where she was spending the holiday. She told him she had no plans yet, but she was positive Melissa would invite her to join her family in Connecticut.

"Would you like to spend Thanksgiving in Long Island with me? First we'll have dinner with my mom, my aunt, and my cousins, then we'll drop in on my dad afterwards. Will Melissa mind if I abduct you on Thanksgiving?"

She smiled at his choice of verb. "I don't think so. Melissa is a fan of yours."

Cara became even more confused now. She confided to Georgia, who could not contain her own excitement.

"He's bringing you to meet his parents? Cara, that's like welcoming you to the family."

Melissa called her the following day to ask about her Thanksgiving plans. She told her about Daniel's invitation, and she could hear Melissa shriek on the other line.

"Cara, how long has this been going on? Why didn't you tell me?"

"Pipe down, Melissa, there's nothing going on. We're just friends."

"He won't invite you if you don't matter to him, so he must have the hots for you, Cara. How exciting!"

* * *

On Thanksgiving, Cara wore a powder blue sleeveless dress with a matching *bolero*, which had tiny embroidery of the same color on its edges and sleeves. Daniel was in a casual beige suit with a pin-striped shirt underneath. He did not wear a tie, yet still managed to look dapper. They arrived in Long Island early evening after a leisurely drive punctuated by small talk and laughter. Daniel's mom lived in the ancestral home where Daniel grew up. When she separated from Daniel's dad, her widowed sister moved in with her. Her sister had two married daughters who came to visit on holidays like this with their respective mates and broods. Thanksgiving was usually a celebrated family affair in their household. Daniel brought two bottles of wine, one each for his mom and dad, and Cara had flowers for his mom.

The first one to greet them was Fudge, Daniel's golden retriever, who was overly excited to see his master. The whole family greeted them warmly as well. Daniel introduced Cara as a friend. There were abundant hugging and kissing, and Cara observed that Daniel was well-loved by his mom, his Aunt Nell, and his cousins Mary and Lesley, who treated him like their own brother. He had two lovable nieces and a nephew he was obviously fond of. Before dinner, Daniel mixed with his cousins' husbands, while Cara stayed with the women, but he checked occasionally to see how she was faring with his family.

Megan Devereaux was a sophisticated woman who did not look like she was in her late fifties, having maintained her figure and her grace. Daniel inherited his dominant features from his mom, including his green eyes.

After partaking of the traditional stuffed turkey, the other dishes, and desserts amidst animated conversation, they retreated to the living room where Daniel's mom showed Cara his baby and early photos.

"Mom, not the one in the birthday suit," Daniel cautioned her.

"Darling, it's all right. You were just a baby then."

His mom showed it to Cara anyway. She looked at it and smiled at him.

"You're so cute." She could see that he already had his good looks even when he was small. There were other photos of him as a boy, as a teenager in basketball and baseball uniforms, and with his friends. He had longish hair in one.

"Isn't he handsome?," his mom said to Cara in open admiration.

"Mommm!," Daniel protested. "You're embarrassing me." Cara was amused.

"Nothing to be embarrassed about, darling. You just happen to be handsome." Daniel just shook his head.

Then it was time to visit Daniel's dad. Robert Devereaux lived by himself, but he had a number of old friends living in the same neighborhood, so he did not get lonely. When he retired, he set up his own motor shop, which was doing well in the area, and keeping him busy. As they said goodbye, Daniel's mom and his Aunt Nell repeatedly told Cara that she was always welcome to come and visit with Daniel.

"Your parents are both residing in Long Island. Don't they ever bump into each other?," Cara asked Daniel when they were in the car.

"No, because my dad lives on the opposite side and they frequent different banks, supermarkets, and stores, so there's a slim chance of an encounter."

"It seems they're both not interested in looking for other partners. Isn't there a possibility of their getting back together again?"

"That would be the greatest gift I can ask for, but it's been seven years, Cara. Their breakup was not even caused by a third party."

"Miracles happen. I'll pray for that."

Daniel's dad was a fine fellow with a sense of humor. He just came in from his brother's home where he was a guest for Thanksgiving dinner. He made Cara laugh with his bag of jokes. He was tall like Daniel and quite strong for his age. He said he jogged everyday for health reasons. Daniel's deep voice, height, and gait were unmistakably from his father's genes.

Cara felt closer to Daniel, especially after meeting his family. She wished he felt the same way. It had been a heartwarming evening for her. She liked Daniel's family, and they made her feel welcomed.

"Your parents are wonderful people," Cara told him on their drive home.

"My mom can be over solicitous, too, sometimes treating me like a baby. You know, she'd call to ask me if I'm taking my vitamins. My gosh, I'm 32 years old!"

"Tell me about it. At my age, I'm still babied, being the girl and the younger one, and constantly reminded by my mother to behave properly."

"So I guess moms are really like that."

"A mother's world revolves around her children. You must understand you're her only child, and she's very proud of you."

"I know."

"Mothers are always instinctively concerned with their children's lives. You can say they're our guardian angels on earth. I know I sometimes get annoyed with constant reminders, but I don't know what I could have become without my mother."

While they were on the road, there was a sudden downpour, followed by successive flashes of lightning and simultaneous claps of thunder.

"It looks like a thunderstorm," Daniel noted.

"Daniel, I have a confession to make. I'm terrified of lightning."

"Don't be afraid, Cara. We're perfectly safe inside the car."

He parked his vehicle on the next shoulder and switched on the emergency lights.

"We'll stay here until this dies down," he told her.

The heavenly occurrence, which some children described as God playing bowling upstairs, continued unabated. Cara closed her eyes and covered her ears with her hands. Daniel acted fast and enfolded her in his arms. Every time lightning flashed, she hid her face in his chest. He stroked and kissed her hair to calm her.

"It's all right. Nothing will happen to us," he whispered reassuringly. She was safe in his arms and felt comforted by him in her moment of fear. After almost half an hour, the rain trickled down, and the lightning and thunder made their exit.

"Thanks. I feel so silly," she told him afterwards while checking her hair.

"Don't feel that way. People have phobias. Next time there's lightning, just holler for me," he told her smiling.

"I think I've created a new action hero," Cara said. "Captain Lightning …who rescues damsels in distress from the horrifying lightning," she delivered the words with flair. They both laughed.

"I don't really know how this fear started," Cara continued. "When I was just a girl, my father would look for me every time there was lightning and hug me. Somehow his hug helped ease the fear."

"I'm a good hugger, too," he assured her, and they laughed again.

"That's not my only fear. I also have claustrophobia. My greatest fear is being trapped in an elevator alone. I remember before when Joey would hug me tightly, I would panic. I was afraid I couldn't breathe, and he used to do that to me playfully. I can't even recall being trapped somewhere when I was small, so I'm wondering where these phobias originated. Do you have one?"

"I don't like snakes. Perhaps you can consider that a phobia of some sort. Well, occasionally I have this fleeting fear of being rejected."

"You, of all people?"

"Believe me. I'm just a regular guy."

They reached Manhattan late evening. He helped her out of his vehicle and accompanied her to the building entrance, enclosing her hand in his. Cara could feel the warmth of his hand course through her own.

"I had a great time. Thank you, Captain Lightning." She meant to tease him, and Daniel was fascinated.

"You have a great sense of humor, Cara. I enjoyed your company, and I believe my family did, too."

He bent his head towards her and planted a soft kiss at the corner of her lips, catching Cara off-guard.

"Goodnight, Cara. Sleep tight."

Cara could not sleep. She kept thinking about that night. She liked being embraced by Daniel. That was almost a kiss from him, and it thrilled her. She imagined what it must be like to be kissed by him on the lips. That night she prayed for his parents' reconciliation.

Chapter

16

Isabel, David's girlfriend, returned to New York on time for Thanksgiving. She went to Colombia for vacation to get acquainted with her cousins there. Her family moved to New York when she was just a small girl, so she was actually more of a New Yorker now than a South American. Nevertheless, she had not forgotten her roots, and they still spoke Spanish in her home. David met her when they were doing a story on the public school system and featured the school in Queens where Isabel used to teach English to Hispanic children. David was immediately smitten by her Latin beauty and vibrant personality. He began calling her and they went out on dates. Before long, they fell in love, and he and Isabel had been a constant twosome since then.

David told Daniel that he wanted Isabel and Cara to know each other. Daniel offered to cook dinner for them at his place, just the four of them, where he said they would be more comfortable. He called up Cara to invite her.

"You're cooking?"

"What's the matter, you don't believe I can cook?"

"You know, Daniel, you're full of surprises."

"There's much more to know about me."

"I can't wait to find out."

"I know I can't get you to come to my place by yourself. We're a foursome, so you're perfectly safe here."

"Are you saying that I'm not safe there alone with you?," she said in a teasing manner.

"That depends," he answered with a hint of mischief in his voice.

What did he mean by that? Cara did not want to pursue this line of conversation, so she quickly changed the subject.

"Do you want me to bring anything, or help you with the cooking maybe?"

"Just bring yourself. I'll manage in the kitchen."

Cara decided to bake a chocolate cake. She bought the necessary ingredients. When Daniel and Isabel came for her, her cake was ready and frosted.

Isabel was a loquacious woman with a lovely face and curls which ran berserk on her brunette head becomingly. Cara took an instant liking towards her. Daniel's place in Central Park west was spacious and tastefully furnished. Its masculine interior was executed in navy blue and light gray. When they arrived at his place, he was already done with his cooking. Too bad, Cara thought, because she would have wanted to see a domesticated Daniel and watch him cook. He was in a taupe T-shirt which revealed some chest hair. Cara noticed and looked away. His maleness disturbed her.

"Did you know I like chocolate cake?," Daniel said to her.

"No. You never told me."

"It happens to be the only kind of cake I eat."

At dinner, they complimented Daniel on his cooking. His baked chicken parmesan, mushroom-garlic-basil pasta, and green salad were worthy of a chef's creation, they all agreed, served with white wine.

"It's perfect." Cara gave it a thumbs-up. "What else can you do, Mr. Devereaux?"

"Ah, that you'll have to find out, Miss Marino." They laughed at his naughty answer.

"You made Daniel smile again, Cara. He's obviously a happier person now," David revealed to her when Daniel left the room to get home-made ice cream. Cara discovered that Daniel liked ice cream. He had an ice cream maker and he made his own low-fat ice cream. They ate it with the chocolate cake.

"Cara, this chocolate cake is delicious. Did you bake it yourself?," Isabel asked.

"Yes. It's a family recipe, which we share with anybody who asks for it."

"So, you cook?"

"I do, and the men in my family, too, but I didn't know American men can cook," she answered, turning to Daniel.

"It was nothing complicated really. I just shove the chicken into the oven and tossed the salad. The pasta was fairly easy. When you live alone, you learn to do many things," Daniel responded.

"Cara, will you teach me how to cook? I still have a lot to learn," Isabel said.

"Sure, Isabel. First you have to know what David wants to eat since you're going to be cooking for your man, right?"

"David doesn't eat much red meat. He prefers chicken and vegetables. He also eats fish and seafood." Isabel cast a glance at David.

"That's easy since there are many chicken and vegetable recipes I can share with you. Let's meet at my place one of these days."

"That's great. Thanks, Cara."

"I'm beginning to like married life already," David commented, beaming.

"Cara, David tells me that you've lived all your life in the Philippines, except when you came here to study. Where did you learn to speak perfect English? You speak like an American," Isabel wanted to know.

"We have fine schools there. English is the medium of instruction from nursery level up to college. We speak English at home. For my bachelor's degree, my major was English. So I think, dream, and breathe in English."

"Do you speak other languages?," Isabel asked.

"Aside from our national language, I can communicate a little in Spanish and Italian. I can practice speaking Spanish with you, Isabel. Let's start right now, but please don't speak too fast. *Tu novio es buen hombre* (Your fiance is a good man)."

"*Tu novio tambien* (Your fiance, too)," Isabel replied.

"*Pero no es mi novio* (But he's not my fiance)." Cara could not help smiling.

"*Es verdad? Que lastima!* (Is that true? What a pity!)." Isabel appeared disappointed.

"Hey, are you talking about us?" David interrupted. The two women laughed.

"Actually, the Philippines is an English-speaking country in Asia and the only Christian country, too," Cara continued. "When you speak English to a Filipino in the street, you're guaranteed a response. That doesn't happen in other Asian countries."

"Like Cara, they also smile a lot," David butted in.

"Filipinos are a happy and resilient people. The Philippines is a third-world country, quite poor, with a weak leadership, but whatever happens, the people always manage to bounce back, still smiling. Filipinos are one of the most misunderstood people, accused of many things and even labeled as dog-eaters. That's just a very small minority there."

"Do they also have your sense of humor?," asked David.

"Oh, yes. Filipinos love to laugh, and they're quite ingenious in crafting jokes. I get a lot of them through e-mail. Why don't I forward them to you?" Cara wrote down their e-mail addresses.

"Are your practices and way of life similar to what we have here?," Daniel questioned.

"You can say we are comparatively more conservative, steep in moral values and family ties. There's no divorce, and many marriages last a lifetime. My parents have been married for 31 years, and my father is even of different nationality. He's Italian."

"Unbelievable," Daniel commented.

"But there are also immoral liaisons even by top government officials. In fact, by comparison, they found your past president's inappropriate behavior mildly amusing there." They laughed at this. "You crack jokes about your president, but with ours, we have volumes of them."

"What kind of climate do you have there?," Isabel asked

"It's a tropical country, so it's particularly hot during summer. We have a lot of lovely beaches especially in the south, where my mother comes from."

"Sounds like paradise," Isabel commented.

"Except for the traffic and the pollution," Cara added.

"Would you leave such a paradise and live elsewhere permanently?," Daniel asked.

"That depends," Cara answered him. They looked at each other and smiled at something the two of them shared from their previous conversation.

"You have a dimple at the right corner of your lips when you smile," Daniel whispered to her. So he noticed her features.

They relaxed in the living room, and Daniel served them brewed coffee, while Chopin was playing in the background. Cara offered to pour and asked David and Isabel how they take their coffee. She did not ask Daniel and just handed him his cup.

"How did you know how I take my coffee?," he asked, surprised.

"I watched you at Starbucks. That's how I take my coffee, too."

Isabel brought her camera. Photography was her hobby, and she preferred taking candid shots while catching her subjects unaware. She and David took turns with the camera. They took shots of Cara, Daniel and Cara together, and the four of them with the use of a timer. The interest level of their conversation never waned.

"When I was in Colombia, everybody was agog over the wedding of a top entertainer," Isabel related. "His name is Pablo Granada. I don't know if you've heard of him, but he's very popular there. He has become wealthy, and he married this beautiful girl from a middle-class family. Grand wedding. The rumor circulating around was that she was asked to sign a pre-nuptial agreement."

"They have such a thing there, too?," Cara asked.

"Yes, but there are conflicting opinions," Isabel continued. "Columbians believe it's an insult to ask your fiancee to agree to a pre-nup because it's like telling her that you're not willing to share what you own, and that's starting your marriage with an absence of trust. What is your opinion about this pre-nup?," she asked them. "It seems to be a common practice here, especially among celebrities."

"It's really how you look at it, Isabel. I'd be the first to suggest the pre-nup if my groom-to-be happens to be rich because I'd want to assure him that I'm marrying him for love, and not for his money," Cara stressed. David nodded slightly and caught Daniel's eye.

"Cara, are you for real?," Daniel asked with astonishment.

"I mean it. I'll always marry for love."

Chapter

17

Fun-loving Filipinos always found reasons to celebrate and get together. There were a number of Filipino associations in New York, and one of them organized a dance benefit to raise funds for the typhoon and flood victims in Central Luzon, the badly battered northern portion of the country. They rallied the Filipinos in New York to attend. Trisha, Josie, and Cristy encouraged Cara to join them. They went stag, except for Trisha. She brought along her husband, who was also Filipino.

The venue was packed. Cara was introduced to some of her countrymen, who had long been New York residents. She met a number of them, some also working at the U.N. Cara, Josie, and Cristy were in demand on the dance floor since there were a lot of single men, but not too many single women. Cara wore a fetching royal blue number. She was a good dancer, and the bachelors there made a queue to dance with her. She was dancing with one of them when Joey tapped her partner on the shoulder to cut in.

"Hi, babe. I'm glad you're here tonight. I was looking around for familiar faces, then I saw you."

"I had no idea you were going to attend this, Joey. Are you with someone?"

"If you mean a date, no. I came with a couple of Filipino doctors from the hospital. How about you? Did you bring your special someone?"

"No. We came stag, too. Why don't you and your friends join our table?"

"Good idea. Maybe we can ward off all those guys wanting to dance with you so we can talk."

Cara and Joey talked the entire evening about a variety of topics. He held her hand and was extremely attentive to her in a manner that signaled the other men there to keep their distance. They danced a couple of times, and Cara felt comfortable in his arms. She missed the closeness they shared before.

"Joey, is there someone special in your life now?"

"There's nobody, babe. Do you know that you're not easy to replace?," he said teasingly.

"C'mon, Joey, you're a good catch. There must be a lot of women eyeing you for a husband. With your good looks, I'm sure you get proposals from women doctors and nurses."

Joey was a good-looking *mestizo*, the type who was attractive to women. His black hair seemed constantly wind-blown which had a sexiness to it. Before, when he attended parties and special occasions, usually with Cara, he would comb it back with a squirt of hair mousse. Cara used to call it his Valentino look.

"I guess I'm not yet ready to get hitched, not with my erratic schedule." As an after-thought, he smiled and added, "If it doesn't work out with you and your special someone, remember I'm still here, babe."

"Joey, stop joking."

"Who's joking?"

* * *

Daniel got a surprise call from his mom one morning. She rarely called him at work. He had just arrived at the office when her call came.

"Mom, is everything all right?"

"Everything is fine, darling. I just have something important to ask you."

"What is it, Mom?"

"Can you drive over tonight? It's really important. I need to see you."

"Mom, are you sure everything is okay? Are you feeling all right?"

"Yes, son. Don't worry. Just come, and I want you to bring Cara along."

"But why? I'll have to ask her first, Mom."

"Tell her we want to see her, too." His mom did not sound worried, and his curiosity was mounting. Is this one of Mom's whims?, he asked himself.

"Okay, if that's what you want. I'll ask her."

"Darling, Cara is a sweet girl. Are you courting her? You seem to like her."

"I do like her, Mom, but I have to proceed slowly. She's not like the other women I've known. Only recently, an unpleasant incident prompted her to stay away from me. I don't want that to happen again."

"Well, good luck, son. I'll see you both tonight."

Daniel immediately phoned Cara at UNDP. Fortunately, she agreed to go with him. She admitted that she was just as curious as he was to find out the reason for his mom's request, which she chose to shroud in mystery. Daniel was confused because his mom was not one to spring surprises. She was usually well-organized and a stickler to regimen, which used to drive him crazy.

"I had your leftover chocolate cake for breakfast this morning. It's still delicious," he told Cara.

"That's not a healthy breakfast, Daniel."

"I know. I'll make up for it. Anyway, I don't eat chocolate cake everyday."

He picked her up at UNDP after work. The drive was never boring to both of them. They found pleasure in talking to each other or listening to CD music they both enjoyed, and singing along with it. They talked about movies they had seen and discussed the plots. They also talked about their favorite TV programs. Cara often watched crime programs and talk shows, and Daniel concurred with her choices. They both enjoyed game shows like *Jeopardy*. They also discovered that they were among the adult avid readers of *Harry Potter*.

"I don't really believe in witchcraft, but this is just fiction. The episodes are very intriguing and the author is highly imaginative. I'm amazed at how she could create out-of-this-world situations and especially those names," Cara remarked.

"I agree it's fun reading, especially the quidditch games. That only shows we're in touch with the child in us," Daniel commented.

"There's a particular book I've long wanted to read – *Ulysses*. Have you read it?", Cara asked him. "It's been rated as one of the greatest novels."

"Yes, by James Joyce. I've read it in College." They made countless discoveries about each other. She told him about Inge and her predicament with her husband.

"I didn't know what to advise her, Daniel. I can't accept infidelity, so it must be best for her to return to

Austria if Bernard would admit to it. Infidelity is a betrayal of trust, so a relationship won't be the same again when a partner is unfaithful. The aggrieved party will require a big heart to be able to forgive. I just pray that Inge will be spared of the pain if there's infidelity involved."

"I admire your concern for your friend, Cara."

As they reached his mom's place, they wondered why it was well-lit and music was playing. Is there a party going on?, Daniel wondered. Fudge met them, wagging his tail vigorously. As they reached the doorstep, the door swung open. Daniel's parents stood there holding hands and smiling at them.

"Dad! Mom! I don't believe this. When did this happen?" They embraced, all three of them. There were tears in Daniel's eyes.

"We bumped into each other yesterday at Target, of all places," his mom explained. "What were you doing this side of town anyway, Bob?" she turned to Daniel's dad.

"I don't know. I just felt like going there. I wasn't thinking of you," he replied to her. "The spark was suddenly rekindled," he related to Daniel and Cara happily.

"I'm so happy for you," Cara told Daniel's parents.

During dinner, Cara learned more about the events of the break-up of Daniel's parents, and then the reconciliation.

"We had a long talk. We realized it was mainly pride. We both didn't want to admit our faults. Come to think of it, our quarrel was nothing serious really, but when I left the house in a huff, I was too proud to come back," Daniel's dad explained.

"It was so silly. Imagine wasting those years," his mom moaned.

"Well, we're going to make up for those lost years, Megan dear. That's a promise," his dad declared. "We attended Mass this morning and asked Fr. Murphy at our parish church to bless our new union. We hope you understand, Daniel, if we didn't tell you earlier. We really wanted to surprise you."

"Of course, Dad. What matters is that you're back together."

"Didn't you miss each other during those years?," Cara wanted to know.

"During the early stage of separation, yes, especially if you're used to sleeping with someone beside you and suddenly his side of the bed is empty," Daniel's mom elaborated. "After time had passed, somehow I got used to it."

"You know how strong-willed she is, so I avoided coming to this area because of my pride. Imagine, it took only one encounter to bring us back together, and I waited this long," his dad added.

"We no longer had a small child since Daniel was already a grown-up, so we thought there was no compelling reason for us to reconcile," his mom continued.

"But I was hurt just the same when you separated. It affected me deeply," Daniel confessed to them.

"We're very sorry, darling," his mom replied, hugging him. "We didn't realize that then." She turned to Cara. "Thank you for praying, Cara. Daniel told me about it. I'm very sure it helped," his mom said.

"There's your gift, Daniel, and it's not even Christmas yet," Cara told him.

After saying goodbye, Daniel took Cara's hand, and they walked to his vehicle holding hands. In her country, holding hands is only for sweethearts. She loved the feel of his hand, and at that very moment, that was all that mattered. A full moon peeked out of a cloud.

"Look at the moon. It's so beautiful," Cara commented.

"I ordered it especially for you," Daniel said jokingly. "Thank you for agreeing to come with me tonight, Cara. It was Mom's idea. She wanted to thank you herself for your prayers," Daniel told Cara.

"I'm glad I came and witnessed a special moment. I can imagine how you felt when your parents separated. I don't know how I'd cope in such a situation."

"I was devastated. It actually changed my life and my whole attitude. When it happened, it made me feel that relationships can crumble. I don't want the same thing to happen to me." He sighed. "I'm glad they're together again. It was partly a default in communication. There's really a great need for openness in marriage."

Daniel was conspicuously happy during their drive back. They talked endlessly, and their topics covered a wide spectrum.

"Next week's topic for *Pulse* is feminism. Are you a feminist, Cara?"

"I'm not a die-hard feminist, but I'm against gender bias, and I agree in giving equal rights to women especially in the workplace. In my country, feminism is not thriving as much as it does here because women somehow get their way. We're really a matriarchal society. The Filipino man may be the recognized head, but the woman rules in many ways. I've seen it work with my parents. My father is the head of the family and makes the major decisions, but my mother is not the passive partner either. She runs our home, manages the finances, and somehow she gets what she wants. I can't really call it wily, but she gets her way in a subtle and loving manner."

"Will you be like that, too, when you get married?"

"I suppose I'd respect my husband more if he'd listen to my opinion without forcing his own. Marriage is a partnership, you know." Daniel was impressed.

"Did you have a good week?," he asked her.

"Yes, I did. I attended this Filipino fund-raising dance event on the prodding of my friends. We had fun."

"Was your ex-boyfriend there?"

"Yes, Joey was there. He actually rescued me from the other guys because there was only a handful of us single women against a horde of bachelors. We were always asked to dance."

Daniel remained silent for half a minute, a worrying thought nagging him which he hurriedly brushed aside.

"Cara is a beautiful name. Does it mean something?," he suddenly asked her.

"It means 'beloved' in Italian. My father chose my name."

"Hmm … so when I say your name, I'm actually calling you 'beloved'? Perhaps I should say your name more often." He cast her a sheepish look, and Cara was tongue-tied. Oh, Daniel, you say the nicest things, she thought.

"Do you know the meaning of your name?," she asked him.

"No." "'Daniel' means 'the Lord is judge'.

"Really? How did you know that?"

"I looked it up in the Bible."

"Thank you for doing that, Cara. So that's what my name means."

It was a lovely night. When they reached Manhattan, it seemed early to part while they were still enjoying each other's company immensely. There was so much to talk about. Daniel parked his vehicle in front of her building, and they decided to walk hand in hand along Manhattan's streets. They did not even notice the Manhattan cacophony, including the police sirens that continuously wailed into the night. It was chilly, so Daniel took off his coat and put it over Cara's shoulders. There were no awkward and silent moments between them. They were totally engrossed in each other's stories that they did not realize it was already past midnight.

"Thanks for your coat," Cara said as he deposited her at her building entrance.

"You're welcome," he answered. Then without warning, he suddenly tilted her chin and kissed her firmly on the lips for a few seconds. It was a brief kiss, but it left Cara weak in the knees.

"Good night, Cara." He smiled at her and left before she could answer.

Chapter

18

At work, Cara's thoughts were on Daniel's kiss. She could still feel the pressure of his lips. Last night she witnessed Daniel cry and it touched her. She wanted to hug and comfort him. They say that real men know how to cry, and she believed that. Later in the day, she got a call from David. He was happy to report that last night Isabel's parents had agreed to give him her hand in marriage. He was in the mood to celebrate and was inviting her and Daniel to dinner.

Cara was on edge. It was getting to be more and more difficult to mask her feelings for Daniel. She always anticipated their meetings and his every call. As she stepped into her apartment after getting home from work, a delivery man came knocking with a bouquet of red roses from Daniel accompanied by a card in his large masculine handwriting which said: *Thank you for your prayers. You taught me to believe in miracles. Always, Daniel.* She kissed his card and said "Daniel, you're so sweet".

Tonight Cara picked her dress with meticulous care. After rummaging through her closet, she finally settled for a body-hugging black bare-back outfit with spaghetti straps which emphasized her full bosom. She wanted to be sexy for Daniel. Just the thought of it excited her. She wore her hair brushed up. She put on her diamond solitaire necklace, a gift from her parents, and diamond earrings. She turned to the mirror and was pleased with her image. David made reservations at a plush Manhattan restaurant. He and Isabel would meet them there. Daniel came to pick up Cara. His face lit up the moment he saw her.

"You're beautiful." His eyes said it all as he stared at her with pure admiration.

"Thank you for the roses. They're lovely," she told him. David and Isabel were already waiting for them when they arrived at the restaurant. Isabel was wearing a provocative red dress. The two behaved like lovebirds, giving each other little pecks and kisses in front of Daniel and Cara.

"Hey, cut it out, you two. Don't make me envious," Daniel told them jokingly.

A voluptuous blonde passed by their table, lingered for a few seconds, and smiled provocatively at Daniel.

"She seems to know you," Cara noted.

"I don't know her from Eve," he whispered back.

"She must find you attractive, Daniel," Isabel said.

"It's nothing new. This usually happens to Daniel in public places," David explained. "Well, we happen to prefer brunettes," he declared, bringing his fist down gently on the table in mock emphasis.

"Thank you," Isabel reacted, lifting her head slightly.

"Could she be one of those women mentioned in that article I read about you?," Cara asked Daniel deliberately, curious to know his reaction.

"What article?"

"Georgia showed me a write-up in a magazine. I don't remember the name of the magazine. It was about you and the women in your life with photos of you with each of them. It had a catchy headline."

"No, she's not one of them, but I know that particular article you're referring to. That was in the past, Cara," he assured her. "There are no other women in my life now." His answer confused her because she was not sure exactly what he meant, and she was reluctant to pry.

While the waiter was pouring their wine, a group of men arrived, and Cara noticed that one of them was Joey. He spotted her and approached their table. He greeted Cara with a kiss on the cheek. She introduced him as her former boyfriend and told them he was a heart surgeon. It confirmed Daniel's guess that he was the guy with Cara at the restaurant.

"I watch your program, Mr. Devereaux. It's very interresting," Joey complimented him. Then he said, "Would you mind if I borrow Cara for a minute?"

"Not at all," Daniel replied.

Joey took Cara's hand and led her to the restaurant foyer, which was visible from where they were seated. They could see Joey taking both Cara's hands in his.

"You look lovely, babe" he said admiringly. "Is he the one?," referring to Daniel.

"He's not yet my boyfriend, Joey, if that's what you mean, but I have feelings for him. We have a lot in common, and he's gentle and kind."

"He seems like a good man. I wish you all the happiness in the world, babe."

"Thank you, Joey. Can I go to you if I have heart problems, doctor?," she asked him in a joking manner.

"You're welcome anytime," he answered touching her cheek. Then he led Cara by the hand back to her table.

"Take care, babe," kissing her on the cheek, and bade the others goodnight.

"He calls you 'babe'? Cara, he's *guapo* and *simpatico*," Isabel commented.

"What does that mean?," David wanted to know.

"It means 'handsome' and 'charming' in Spanish," Isabel translated.

"He's a doctor, and he's just used to his bedside manners," Cara explained.

"He seems young to be a surgeon," Isabel commented.

"He's 30, like my brother."

"Do all Filipino men look like that?," Isabel asked.

"Not all. Joey is exceptional," Cara answered.

Daniel did not say a word, but inside him the embers of jealousy began to smolder. What is happening to me?, he asked himself. He was never jealous of anyone before. Their food arrived and they enjoyed it amidst talk and banter. Then a quartet of guitarists started to play and sing Spanish songs, to Isabel's delight and Cara's, too.

"Spanish songs are beautiful and very romantic. Spanish is one of the romance languages, you know. Do you think I can request them to sing a favorite of mine?," Cara asked David.

"I'm sure they'll oblige," David answered. He called one of the waiters and handed him the piece of paper where Cara wrote the name of the song. The leader of the quartet nodded his head and they proceeded to sing.

"It's dedicated to you, Daniel. The song is *Ojos Verdes*, which means 'green eyes'," Cara told him.

"It's beautiful," Isabel commented, understanding the words of the song. "Latin lovers are very passionate."

Cara closed her eyes as she listened, conscious of the man sitting beside her with green eyes. She was grateful when the quartet repeated the song because she never tired of listening to it.

"Thank you, Cara. I like the music, but I want to understand the words. Do you think you can write down the translation for me?," Daniel requested.

Cara knew the words by heart. With Isabel's help, she wrote down the translation on paper provided by the waiter. Daniel was pleased with what he read. After the quartet, a pianist took over and played dance music. Some couples took to the dance floor. David asked Isabel to dance, so Cara and Daniel were left alone.

"I'm going to London this coming week with David and our team for an interview with the British Prime Minister. I'll call you from there," he told her.

"Will you have time for that?"

"I'll find time for you, Cara," he assured her.

"That's Glenn Miller's *Moonlight Serenade*," Cara commented when the next piece was played. There were more couples on the dance floor now.

"C'mon, let's dance." He took her hand as he guided her towards the dance floor.

Moonlight Serenade always had a romantic effect on Cara since she was very young. In high school, she and her friends discovered that they shared the same sentiments. It was one particular piece they wanted to dance to with someone they really liked and cherished, even if it was music from their parents' time. When it was played during their parties, they kept wishing that their crushes would ask them to dance. In Daniel's arms, Cara was lost in reverie. She dreamed of being locked in his embrace, and this was it, sending her heart racing. It was different during the lightning incident because she was scared, but now she was fully conscious of her senses. His nearness and the scent of his cologne were intoxicating. She felt the strength of his body against hers. His chin touched her temple, and she thought he must feel her rapid heartbeat. "What's your perfume?," he asked her.

"It's called *Diorissimo*. It's an old scent."

"I like it. It's very feminine."

He brought her hand to his lips, then he bent his head and stole a kiss on her nape, transmitting currents through Cara's body. His hand moved along her bare back, which sent shivers down her spine. Then he looked deeply into her eyes and put her hand against his chest where she could feel the quick rhythm of his heart. Their eyes locked together with repressed emotions. If this could only go on forever, she dreamed.

The eyes were the first thing that attracted Cara to a man. She felt magnetized by Daniel's green eyes, which could be piercing in one moment then soulful in the next. She used to admire Joey's hazel almond-shaped eyes, which he inherited from his Spanish mother. The music stopped and Daniel and Cara did not even notice until David and Isabel passed them.

"Hey, lovebirds, the music is over," David told them, tapping Daniel on the shoulder.

They left the restaurant holding hands and waited at the hotel entrance for the valet attendants to bring their cars when a camera flashed. A photographer took a picture of Daniel and Cara, then left hurriedly. Daniel was worried and he frowned.

"Maybe it was just a fan of yours," David assured him.

Daniel was very quiet as he drove Cara home. He reached for her hand with his right hand, holding it tightly while steering the wheel with his left.

"Daniel, you're driving," Cara cautioned him gently. So he put her hand on the steering wheel and covered it with his own, and they both laughed at his alternative. When they reached her apartment building, he turned to Cara inside the car.

"I have to do this," he said. He drew her to him and found her lips. He kissed her intensely, then suddenly released her. Cara was still recovering from the intensity of his kiss when he went around to open the car door for her. She was in a daze as he escorted her to the building entrance. They stood there facing each other, the green depths of his eyes holding hers captive. Then Daniel took her in his arms and sought her lips again. He kissed her gently at first, starting slowly on her upper lip then moving down to her lower lip. Daniel's caressing movements with his lips drove Cara's emotions uphill, and she found herself responding ardently to his kisses.

"Cara, Cara," he whispered hoarsely, while kissing her passionately now.

Cara felt weak and could not move from where she stood when Daniel turned to go. He almost reached his car when he decided to turn back towards her and kissed her hard once more.

"I'll call you," he told her. It took several minutes before Cara could bring herself up to her apartment. She was shaken but ecstatic. She could not utter a word while Daniel was kissing her. His effect on her was paralyzing. Now she knew what it was like to be kissed by Daniel. It was heaven. Joey was the only guy who had ever kissed her until now, and Daniel's brand of kisses was beyond compare.

* * *

"How are things between you and Cara," David asked Daniel during a break in the discussion of their London itinerary.

"It's getting better everyday," Daniel answered smiling.

"You've been looking quite happy lately. Are you in the intimate stage now?"

"No, just kissing. The other night after our dinner, I couldn't help myself. I kissed her hard, and she responded."

"That's a positive development, Daniel."

"I can't go farther than that. She made it clear that she's not in favor of premarital sex. If I want to win her, I have to respect that."

"I know she's Catholic. Isabel is, too, but I know a lot of New York Catholics who are not that morally strict. You're one of them," he reminded him. "Well, it must be her upbringing and the Asian in her."

"That's what makes her different. She has this childlike innocence which makes me want to protect her. I've never met anyone like her, David."

"My friend, I think you've been hit by the thunderbolt like Michael Corleone."

Chapter

19

Cara's moral upbringing steered her towards keeping herself chaste. She did not realize that she would be wrestling with her inner self on the issue. When she was with Daniel, and he kissed her the way he did, it became extremely difficult for her not to surrender completely to her overpowering emotions. Restraint is a virtue when one is deeply in love with someone since love's compelling journey usually takes the natural path towards full expression. Premarital sex is a very strong issue in a woman's life in her country. Sex is held sacred. At an early age, women are made to understand that it is an act reserved for marriage because it represents exclusivity and permanence. Daniel was a great and honorable man in Cara's estimation because he respected her, and he did not attempt to go beyond kissing her.

Cara had her sessions on the birds and the bees with her mother during early girlhood. She was an inquisitive young girl and was not hesitant in asking intimate questions, which her mother managed to answer satisfactorily, but she had never seen a man in "full monty", except Vince. Their bedrooms on the second story of their home had a door which was locked from the rest of the house when they were inside. It was their private enclave with a family room in the middle. When Cara was 11, she and her mother were sitting in the family room when Vince came out nonchalantly from the bathroom totally unclad and asking for an extra towel. Their mother scolded him for exposing himself in Cara's presence, but Cara found it funny. Naughty as she was at that age, she teased Vince, "I saw it, I saw it. It's got hair." Except for that incident, her knowledge of a man's anatomy was limited to pictures when she, Melissa, and their friends would sneak issues of *Playgirl* and secretly scrutinize the photos of hunks in their frontal glory.

Fortunately, December was a lean month at UNDP because Cara simply could not work. She was reeling from the dizzying effects of love. Yes, now she was fully certain she was in love with Daniel. He was the only man she wanted to be with. She ached for him body and soul. It was already winter, and she knew that the coldness of winter would be unbearable without Daniel. He left for London with the *Pulse* team, and she was already missing him terribly, knowing he was miles away. She asked Georgia to go out to lunch, and she shared with her the events of her love life.

"Cara, he's obviously in love with you."

"Oh, Georgia, I hope so because I know now for sure that I love him and he's the only man I want to love, but I'm confused. He hasn't told me he loves me. Why?"

"He will, trust me. His actions point to that. Look, he brought you twice so far to Long Island to his family, and you've been his exclusive date. As far as I know, he's not dating other women. How he treats you and the way he behaves when he's with you are clear signs that he loves you. Maybe he's just being cautious, and he respects you. You must have told him something that's making him behave with restraint and caution."

"Well, I told him I don't favor premarital sex and live-in arrangements."

"There you are. I admire him for respecting you, Cara. He's some guy."

"Do you think it has nothing to do with my being half-breed? You know, I'm partly from the brown race."

"Daniel Devereaux doesn't strike me as a man who would consider that as an obstacle."

"Well, he told me he's not racist."

Georgia admired him all the more for that. "Is he a good kisser?," She asked Cara teasingly..

"The best. Have you seen Richard Gere kiss in the movies? In that same intense fashion. I've never experienced anything like it. Oh, Georgia, I feel helpless when Daniel kisses me."

Wow, I can just imagine what it's like to be kissed by Daniel Devereaux."

* * *

Daniel invaded Cara's thoughts the whole day. As she got home from work, she called Melissa and confessed to her.

"Melissa, I'm in love."

"With Daniel Devereaux, I'm sure."

"Yes. I'm lovesick and I can't concentrate on my work. He's in London now and I miss him very much. Melissa, what will I do?"

"Oh, Cara, I'm deliriously happy for you that you've found your man. Did you have sex with him?"

"You should know me better than that, Melissa," Cara scolded her.

"Just joking, Cara. I know you."

"We just kissed, and it was wonderful. Why is it that a kiss seals the truth? When Daniel kissed me, I knew for certain that I love him. He hasn't declared his feelings for me, and that's what bothers me, Melissa."

"Some men don't say those three little words right away, Cara, but it doesn't mean that they don't. Maybe he's just waiting for the right time to tell you."

"I hope you're right because I can't wait to let him know how I feel. I'm not going to make the first move. That's not me."

"I know, Cara. Tell me more about the kissing," Melissa prodded her.

"It felt like heaven. He really knows how to kiss. He awakened something in me I didn't know I was capable of feeling, and I kissed him back. I have to get off the phone now, Melissa, because he promised to call me from London. I want to hear his voice."

"Wow, you're really in love, Cara. Talk to you later."

In a matter of minutes Cara's phone rang. It was Daniel just as she anticipated.

"Miss me?," he asked with mischief in his voice.

"Yes." She tried not to sound too eager.

"I miss kissing you." The desire in his voice was transparent even if he was miles away. She closed her eyes as their kissing episode flooded her mind.

"How did the interview go?," she asked him to deviate from her thoughts.

"It went very well. The Prime Minister is an enigmatic personality. We'll be back there day after tomorrow after wrapping up here. The guys have something lined up for tomorrow. Don't worry, I'm behaving like a saint," he told her laughing.

"Just be back, Daniel. Say hello to your team for me."

"I'll do that. Bye, Cara. I miss you."

Cara could not help going over their phone conversation and relishing his words. He told her he missed kissing her, and he said "I miss you" in parting.

* * *

At 25, Cara had never been genuinely in love before. In her teens, she had a series of crushes on her professors, basketball players, and cute university guys, just like any young girl. What she had with Joey was a comfortable relationship which grew from familiarity. She could not recall having been in a passion-charged situation with him. She remembered feeling comfortable in his arms. They hugged a lot even in front of her parents, who trusted Joey not to take advantage of her. She loved to snuggle up to him, and they kissed often. Now she realized that they were innocuous kisses. Joey was a wonderful guy, and she still had special feelings for him. Cara knew that he would be perfect husband material, but it was Daniel who made her heart flutter.

* * *

Inge told Cara the next time they met that Bernard admitted his indiscretion. Cara felt her pain. In tears, Inge related their encounter. There was no shouting, no harsh words, and he was very apologetic. He claimed it was just a temporary liaison when he yielded to one of his students who flirted with him. Still it caused Inge considerable heartache. She told him that she needed to get away. He begged her not to go, but Inge told him that she had to do it to keep her sanity. He could not leave with her because he had to finish his contract with the university.

"If he truly loves you, he'll go after you," Cara told Inge.

"At the moment, I don't really care. I just want to go home."

"Will you accept him if he wants to come back to you?"

"I guess so. I still love him, but our relationship will need a lot of healing."

"I'll pray for you, Inge."

"Thank you, Cara. You're a true friend."

Before Inge left for Vienna, she and Cara met once more. Inge looked less harried in anticipation of her trip and her eagerness to see her family. She handed Cara a piece of paper.

"Inge, what's this?," Cara asked.

"Just a few lines I wrote for you in one of my creative excursions."

It read: *Lines to Cara: Who showed that though lives can brush by each other so hurriedly, one can stop and patiently listen to part of a part of a heart that's another's.*

"Inge, this is lovely. I'll always treasure this. Thank you very much."

"I'll never forget you, Cara."

"You'll always be my friend, Inge, and I expect to hear from you. Remember, this is the age of technology and e-mail."

"How's your love life coming along?"

"We're closer now as we're getting to know each other better, but there's no commitment."

"In time, Cara. You deserve a good man."

Chapter

20

Cara stopped by the newsstand on her way to work and got the shock of her life. On the front page of the National Inquirer was her picture with Daniel. She hurriedly bought a copy and took it with her. She read it in the privacy of her cubicle. The article insinuated that women were interested mainly in Daniel's stature and worth. She was named and identified as an Asian and his constant companion. She felt lumped among those women who were after him for what he was worth, and it was not flattering. It divulged Daniel's annual salary at GCN which amounted to seven figures, excluding bonuses and perks. It pictured him as a moneyed eligible bachelor. That photographer at the restaurant entrance who stole the shot must have provided the photo. Daniel was right worrying about him at the time.

Cara rested her head on her desk and wept. Luckily she was by herself at that time of the morning. After some time, she showed Georgia the article. Georgia sympathized with her and comforted her.

"I know how you feel, Cara, but don't worry because few people believe what the tabloids write about. They just read them out of curiosity."

"But it paints me as a gold digger, and I'm not that."

"I know, and Daniel knows that, too."

"How did they know my name?," she asked perplexed.

"They're very resourceful. You'd be surprised."

"This is really hurting me and Daniel, so I think it's best that we stay away from each other for a while."

"Do you think he'll agree?"

"He should. I'll be suggesting this to protect him."

* * *

Her phone was ringing as she opened the door to her apartment. It was Vince calling from Chicago.

"Cara, I read the National Inquirer."

"You have time to read that tabloid?" Suddenly she feared her brother's reaction.

"One of the nurses showed me a copy when she saw your name and asked if you're any relation to me. What's the meaning of this, Cara? How did you get involved with this Daniel Devereaux? How long has this been going on?" Vince sounded angry.

"Vince, please don't be angry with me. I'm hurt enough as it is. I'm dating him, but we're not romantically involved. We had dinner when this photographer stole a shot. That's how it got to the tabloid. They made a story out of it since Daniel is hot copy."

"Cara, it puts you in a bad light. You should know better than to get entangled with a celebrity. You should have stayed with Joey. He's right for you."

"I know my own heart, Vince. Daniel is a great guy. He's not in New York right now, so I don't know his reaction to the article and if he has read it."

"I can imagine what our parents would feel if they read the article. Eventually they'll find out because somebody is bound to tell them. This is what I think I'll do. I'll call and warn them about this so they'll know the real story beforehand. That should sort of cushion the impact."

"Thanks, Vince. I really appreciate this. You've really nothing to worry about. Daniel is a gentleman. I hope you'll meet him. He and Joey have already met."

"Yeah? and Joey doesn't mind?"

"No. It's long been over between us."

"Just be careful, Cara. I love you and I care about what happens to you."

"Thank you for caring. I love you, too."

* * *

While Cara was on the bus on her way to work the following morning, two women boarded and took the seats behind her. At first she did not mind their conversation. They tried to speak in whispers, but she overheard them mention Daniel's name and the National Inquirer item.

"He should really be careful whom he keeps company with because most likely it's his fame and fortune they're after," said the first woman.

"Right. With his looks alone, he can choose any woman. Most of those women are only interested in what he's worth," the second one added.

"He has to be more careful, especially with foreigners" the first woman concluded.

Cara was relieved when they got off the bus. She shared the incident with Georgia.

"There's so much racism in this country. Do you experience this?," she asked Georgia.

"Everyday, my dear, but I just have to live with it. There's not much I can do about it. I live in this country."

"I observe the way African-Americans and people of other races are regarded, based on the color of their skin. We all happen to be human beings. Those women were insinuating that I'm interested only in Daniel's money. I'm not even aware of Daniel's financial assets, and I don't care what he owns. Money is not, and never will have any relevance to my falling in love."

"You're admirable, Cara. Those people have shallow minds. Don't allow them to affect you." Georgia advised her.

* * *

"Well, look who's here. It's the Asian muse." It was Madeline, the last person Cara expected to see in the grocery store. She enunciated the word 'Asian' maliciously. Cara could sense that she was up to her devious plan. Cara wanted to avoid her, but she was next in line at the check-out cashier. She decided that her best defense against mean people like Madeline was mute reaction. Verbal abuse was not Cara's kind of battle.

"It certainly got you on the front page of the National Inquirer. This is bad for Daniel's career. Tsk, tsk," Madeline continued to castigate her, and she wanted the others waiting in line to hear. It attracted the attention of the people in the queue, but Cara just ignored her.

"Have a nice day," Cara told everyone there before leaving, giving them her winsome smile. They all responded positively, including the grocery personnel who knew her. Madeline got a deserved it-serves-you-right stare from them, and it silenced her.

Chapter

21

One of the *Pulse* staff showed Daniel a copy of the tabloid the minute he arrived from London. He called Cara right away, and she was happy to hear his voice.

"Cara, how are you? I suppose you've seen the National Inquirer. I'm sorry about that article. I was raving mad when I read it."

"You don't have to apologize, Daniel. It's not your fault."

"I know, but somehow I feel responsible. My initial reaction was to get back at them, but our lawyers here say it won't do any good. They're suggesting I just ignore it. I'm concerned about you, Cara. I don't want you hurt by a false story."

"I'm okay. I'm more concerned about you. Maybe we should avoid seeing each other for a while so they'll have nothing to talk about. To be safe, maybe we shouldn't even call each other."

"Is that what you want? For how long?"

"I don't know, but it's an alternative. I want to protect you, Daniel."

"I should be the one protecting you, Cara, but if this is what you believe we should do, can we discuss it? I'm going over there after dinner. I'm having dinner with some network executives, so it will be after that. Okay with you?"

"Yes. I'll wait for you."

Cara did not feel like eating dinner. She was too anxious to see Daniel. She fixed a sandwich and forced herself to finish it just to fill her stomach. She passed the time watching TV, but her mind continued to wander to Daniel. He arrived before 10:00. When she saw him, she realized how much she missed him. He looked handsome in his dark suit. She went freely into his open arms and wished she could stay there forever.

"I miss you, Cara," he told her. He kissed her forehead, then her mouth and lingered there. She was lost in the pleasure of his kiss.

"Let's sit down and talk before I stray from my purpose," he said. "First, let me give you something I found for you during my trip." He handed her a package. Cara opened it. It was a copy of *Ulysses*.

"Wow, where did you find this? Thanks a lot. How was your dinner?"

"Good. It was a culmination of an earlier meeting where we assessed *Pulse* and discussed a possible new format. David was with us."

He took her hand and led her to the living room where they sat facing each other. Daniel leaned close to her, took both her hands in his, and looked into her eyes.

"Now, what's this about not seeing or calling each other? Is that what you really want?," he asked her in a gentle tone, which melted Cara's heart.

"Maybe if they don't see us together, the gossip will die down and they'll have nothing to talk and write about," Cara explained.

"You said you want to protect me. What do you mean by that?"

"Daniel, you're the celebrity. It may hurt your career. I'm just an ordinary person."

"You're far from ordinary, Cara. You're very special." Cara felt good hearing him say that.

"I don't quite agree with your suggestion, but if it makes you happy... How long do you have in mind?," he asked.

"For a month at least?"

"That long?" He sounded disappointed. "Okay, one month then before you change your mind and make it longer. It's not going to be easy. Again, I'm sorry for putting you through this. Did you have uncomfortable or awkward moments with people you know when the article came out?"

"Well, my Filipino friends all thought it was a malicious story. Georgia, my African-American friend at UNDP, was quite supportive and assured me that people don't really believe everything in the tabloids. My brother called from Chicago and he was angry at first. I related to him how it happened, and he understood. He'll call our parents to warn them about it since that tabloid is sold there, and they'll find out somehow, but I'm sure they'll understand, too. Vince scolded me for going out with you, but I told him you're a great guy and a gentleman."

"Am I really all that to you?," he asked, looking at her with a smile on his lips. Cara felt herself blush and managed a timid smile.

"You're blushing. I like that. Maybe you should rest now. I know this has been difficult for you. So, we'll see each other again a month from today?" She nodded. He did not seem too happy. He sighed and said, "I guess it's time to say goodbye then."

He rose and helped her to her feet. Cara marveled at how tall he was. He took her in his embrace. He held her long, not wanting to let her go, and Cara didn't mind staying in his arms regardless of time. Then he looked deeply into her eyes and lowered his gaze to her lips. He touched them with his fingers, moving lightly over them and tracing their outline. It was a loving and intimate gesture to Cara and she felt herself weakening. Then he kissed the spot where her dimple was and his lips traveled to her cheek before seeking her mouth. He ravished her lips with a hunger he had been restraining. Cara was aware only of the emotions he stirred in her and yielded to his kiss with her whole being. At that very moment, nothing else mattered to her but Daniel. He released her after a long time, and they were both breathless. He caressed her cheek with his hand and looked at her lovingly, his green eyes replete with tenderness.

"Goodbye, darling. I'll miss you." He moved towards the door and departed without looking back, leaving Cara dumbfounded. She had to sit down to steady herself. She was already feeling his absence, and it made her cry.

"I love you, Daniel," she whispered in tears. It warmed her heart that he called her 'darling'.

Days after, Cara could not dismiss Daniel from her thoughts. No matter how she tried to keep herself busy, his face kept intruding into her wakefulness. She recalled the message from the fortune cookie in the Chinese restaurant which advised her, *listen to your heart and balance it with reason*. She realized that was what she was doing.

* * *

"Daniel, we're getting a flood of requests for you to guest in a number of shows. It's about time we discuss this," David told him.

"I don't really like doing that, David. For what particular reason? If it's for the sake of our program, we don't need to promote it. Not for myself either. That's the last thing I want. You know I'm a very private person. They'll delve into my private life, and I certainly don't want that. Then they'll start asking why I'm not yet married. Cara may even get dragged into it. Please say no to them for me, will you?"

"I'll see what I can do. You're really something else, Daniel. Some people are scrambling to guest in TV shows, and you're just the reverse. What about Larry King? What we said to him earlier was as good as a promise for you to be interviewed by him."

"Okay, we'll keep our word with Larry. We owe him that."

* * *

The interview on *Larry King Live* took place in New York the following week and went very well. Larry King began the interview by giving credit to Daniel's accomplishments and popularity. It turned out to be an animated dialogue between the interviewer and the interviewee. Daniel responded to Larry's questions satisfactorily, elaborating on his answers. Towards the end of the one-hour program, Larry, in his usual casual manner, asked Daniel a question he could not sidetrack.

Larry asked, "I'm aware you want your private life to be just that, private, but I can't resist asking you just one more question. You may choose to answer it or not. You're considered New York's most eligible and elusive bachelor, and you've been linked with a number of women. By this time, have you found your ideal woman?"

Daniel smiled slightly, more out of amusement. "Okay, I'll answer that, Larry. Yes, I have, and that's all I will tell you."

"I can understand that, Daniel. I'm sure some of our TV viewers, the women especially, are not too happy about it." Larry King did not delve any further.

* * *

Vivian, Daniel's secretary and assistant, put through to him a call from Greg Lonsdale, executive vice-president for programming of Cardinal Broadcasting Corporation.

"Hi, Greg, it's good to hear from you. What can I do for you?," Daniel asked.

"How are you, Daniel? We haven't had the chance to talk longer at the Emmys. How about lunch?"

"That's fine with me, Greg. Just set the date."

"Congratulations on your program. It's leading in the ratings. I'm proud of you."

"You're doing very well yourself. You're EVP there now."

"Well, at my age, I have to get somewhere," he answered with a chuckle.

Greg Lonsdale used to be a vice-president at NBC. Daniel had brief encounters with him when he was still working with the network. He liked Greg Lonsdale because he was kind and always had a good word for everybody. He was what they called a "people person". At the helm at CBC, he had effected a number of notable improvements in their programming.

Daniel had no inkling why Lonsdale invited him to lunch. He was therefore completely surprised when he offered him a job. Lonsdale admitted that television was a competitive arena and Daniel was acknowledged as the best interview host. CBC would conceptualize a new show for him if he would hop into their wagon. It would be in the same league as *Pulse*, and Daniel was their first choice to host it. He would have free rein with the program format, plus a more-than-generous salary package prepared for him. In other words, he was being pirated. Daniel told Lonsdale that he was flattered that they considered him and thanked him for the offer. He promised to weigh everything carefully and give him his answer in a week's time at the longest.

Such an offer was good for one's ego, but Daniel had already made up his mind. He was happy with what he was doing and he liked his team. He was earning more than enough. He was comfortable with David as his executive producer, and he had no immediate plans of moving out of GCN. After three days, he called up Greg Lonsdale and explained to him tactfully why he was declining the offer.

Chapter

22

Cara went about her work with a degree of reluctance. She felt like life was sucked out of her and she often found herself staring into nothingness in her lugubrious state. She sought comfort in reliving her last encounter with Daniel and remembering their tender moments. She reminisced on the times they spent together.

They ran in tandem in Central Park and made regular visits to the abandoned children's center. They played tennis at the sports club where Daniel was a member. He was much too good a player to beat. She had not played for ages, and her game was pretty rusty. They visited museums, attended exhibits, ate ice cream while strolling in Central Park, and frequented Starbucks for their usual coffee and latte. He even insisted on accompanying her to see Melissa in Connecticut because he wanted to meet someone from her family. On rainy days, they enjoyed browsing in bookstores. The music that they enjoyed together was the most haunting for her. Every time she heard the songs they shared, she succumbed to an unfathomable loneliness, as if the words were written intentionally for her, and they were able to read her heart.

They watched *Miss Saigon* on Broadway even if both of them had seen it before because he was awed by the Filipino talents in the cast. The principal character Kim had almost always been played by a Filipina. She enjoyed every minute with him, and she had never been happier. Cara contented herself with watching *Pulse* when it was aired. She watched the Larry King interview. Both Georgia and Melissa told her excitedly that she was the woman Daniel referred to, but still she was not sure because they were not even committed to each other. Seeing Daniel on TV was the closest she could get to him. So this is what love is. In the absence of the beloved, there can only be pain, Cara realized, and she was experiencing it now.

During their period of separation, she received an e-mail message from him which said: *Dear Cara, We did not agree not to communicate by e-mail. Anyway, I'm taking the chance just to let you know that I miss you. Love, Daniel.* Then he quoted from Shakespeare's Sonnet 116: *'Let me not to the marriage of true minds admit impediments. Love is not love which alters when it alteration finds.'* She interpreted it as a suggestion from him not to be fazed by adversity, with a vague admission of his love for her. Cara pondered over his e-mail and its underlying message. Was she reading it right?

* * *

During one of her regular calls to her parents, her mother expressed her fears about her involvement with Daniel. They had already known about the tabloid article.

"Cara, you hardly know this man. Vince tells us he's a celebrity. I'm worried about you, *hija*."

"Mama, there's nothing to worry about. Daniel is a real gentleman, and he hasn't taken advantage of me, if that's your concern. Besides, we're not involved, and we're just dating. Mama, remember you told me that when I meet a man I should look at his childhood because you said that what he was as a child has a great bearing on what he is as an adult?"

"That's right."

"Daniel had a happy childhood. He has wonderful parents. They were separated for seven years and recently got back together again. I've met them. And, Mama? He's Catholic." Filipinos, in general, regard religion as a vital factor in a relationship.

"I'm glad to hear that, Cara. I just want you to remember to use your head, not just your heart."

"Your words are already ingrained in me, Mama. You know that."

"I know, *hija*, but sometimes we have moments of weakness. I just don't want you to get hurt. A broken heart is the hardest to mend. Please heed my advice. Take care of yourself now. Love you. Here's your Papa."

"Cara, how's my girl?," her father asked.

"I'm fine, Papa. How are you? How's your health?"

"Fine, sweetie. Your Mama and I take regular walks within the subdivision, and we're both in good shape. We still swim and play tennis regularly."

"That's good, Papa. Keep it up."

"Cara, just be careful there. New York is not like Manila or Makati."

"But I've lived here before, remember?," she quickly reminded him.

"Yes, but it was different then, sweetie, because Vince was there to look after you. You're living independently now. Just listen to your Mama's advice. Okay?"

"Thank you for your concern, Papa. I don't want you to worry. I'll never do anything that will hurt you."

"That's good. Take care, sweetie. We love you."

"I love you, too."

Parental concern could be annoying in a way, but Cara knew that it was an expression of their unwavering care and love for her. It was typically Filipino.

* * *

"Cara, can you accompany me to go to Price Club in Long Island?," Melissa invited her. "There's an item Keith needs which is available there, and I offered to get it for him. You should go out to keep your mind off Daniel."

"But, Melissa, Daniel goes home to Long Island on weekends."

"Yeah, but what are the chances of his going to Price Club? C'mon. It will do you good. Besides, I want to have someone to talk to while I'm driving, and it might as well be you. I miss you, Cara."

"Okay, Melissa. Maybe you can cheer me up. You always do."

On the drive to Long Island, Cara poured out her heart in between tears to Melissa, who was like a sister to her. Melissa understood her because she knew Cara thoroughly since childhood. Cara had always been a sensitive and caring person, and Melissa's heart went out to her.

"Cara, It pains me to see you like this. I'm sure this will all be straightened out in due time. You'll see."

"I love him very much, Melissa. I've never felt this way before. It wasn't like this at all when Joey and I parted."

"Daniel apparently loves you, too, Cara. I've seen the way he looked at you. I'm positive you're that woman he was referring to during Larry King's interview."

"I don't know, Melissa, but I do know I miss him terribly. I feel empty without him. Right now I'm on automatic pilot. I desire to know everything about him. Like, what part of the chicken does he prefer and what does he eat for breakfast? I still don't know all his favorite foods. Does he have any pet peeves? What are his habits? I want to be familiar with his moods. I don't even know if he has a temper because I've never seen him angry. The only time he seemed angry was when he learned about the National Inquirer article. I want to know his favorite things. What are his dreams? I want to be part of them. I know we're compatible. We enjoy the same things, but I still don't know everything about him."

"There's more. Does he wear boxer shorts or briefs?" This made Cara laugh a little.

"Melissa, you're really funny."

"At least I made you laugh. Cara, remember how we used to swoon over the intense type of men, like Brad Pitt and Antonio Banderas? Well, my Keith is not really the intense type, but Daniel is the exact guy we dreamed about when we were younger."

"Yes, you're right. Melissa, in your case, was there ever any problem with your being different from Keith?" Melissa was three-quarters Filipino and had a darker skin than Cara.

"Never between the two of us, but occasionally when we're in a public place, we still get those stares and hear unfavorable comments. I guess the difference is more pronounced in our case since Keith is blond. It doesn't really bother us anymore."

"What concerns me is that this racial issue will always surface because Daniel is a popular figure. It won't be good for him, and I may not be good for him either."

"Hey, don't think in those terms, Cara. You never had any problem with self-esteem."

"I guess you're right."

"Although it'll be a different situation for you. Since Daniel is not just any ordinary guy, people will always find room for criticizing his choice."

"Once again, it reverts to race," Cara countered.

"Well, that's purely Daniel's business and none of theirs."

They could see that Price Club had its usual heavy weekend crowd, but they were not really there to shop. They found Keith's item, and some other useful and reasonably priced ones while walking through the aisles.

"Cara, what are you doing here? How are you?" It was Daniel's mom, and she was pleased to see Cara.

"I didn't expect to see you here, Mrs. Devereaux. This is my cousin Melissa. I accompanied her to get something that's available here."

"Does Daniel know you're here? He's at home now. Why don't you come over to the house and surprise him?"

"I don't think that's a good idea, Mrs. Devereau. Didn't he tell you? We agreed not to see each other for a while."

"Oh, I'm sorry to hear that, Cara." Megan Devereaux appeared surprised and disappointed. "He hasn't said a word about it. So, that's why he's been so quiet, and he doesn't seem to be himself lately. Do you want me to mention to him that we saw each other?"

"I guess it's okay. Please say hello to him for me, Mrs. Devereaux."

"What do you make of that, huh?," Melissa asked after Daniel's mom left. "I believe your prince misses you." Cara would like to believe that, too.

Cara spent the weekend with Melissa in Connecticut. She felt she needed to be with family, and Melissa was her nearest relative. She understood Cara and had a way of making her feel better. They went window shopping and strolling in Manhattan before returning to her apartment. They entered several stores, including Tiffany's to admire the diamonds on display, pointing to each other their favorite pieces.

* * *

When Cara checked her e-mail, there was a message from Daniel. He wrote: *Dear Cara, Thank you for saying hello to me through Mom. That's thoughtful of you. Your emotional bank account must be filled to the brim. When I hear your name mentioned, it's when I realize how much I miss you. I hope you're all right. Take care. Love, Daniel.* Cara felt consoled that at least there was some form of communication from him. This was the second time he signed 'Love, Daniel'. Do people normally sign 'Love'?, she asked herself.

A week had passed which sliced off a portion of their one-month pact of not seeing each other. Cara received a box of chocolates from Daniel with a note: *To Cara, in celebration of a week gone by. Three weeks to go. Love, Daniel.* He was counting.

* * *

"Daniel, I know now who's been feeding the tabloids with unpleasant items about you and Cara," Vivian said.

"There's another blind item which came out today and it's rather unflattering to Cara."

"But who in heaven's name would do that, Viv?," Daniel asked, frowning.

"Madeline, that's who. I overheard her telling one of the girls in the ladies' room. She didn't know I was inside one of the cubicles. She was saying that she knows a lot of reporters. She was practically admitting that she gave out the information to them. Her parting words were 'Daniel should see the light soon'."

"What is she trying to do?"

"Can't you see? She's trying to discredit Cara. She wants you, Daniel."

"Well, that's not going to change anything,"

"Beware of her, Daniel. I never liked that woman. She's really bitchy."

"She can do whatever she wants. It won't alter how I feel towards Cara."

Chapter

23

Isabel asked Cara to be her bridesmaid. The wedding was set in two weeks. Cara was honored that Isabel wanted her to be part of her bridal entourage. Daniel would be David's best man. It meant that they would see each other before their one-month pact expired, and she was already anticipating it. That same week, she had her measurements taken by the dressmaker, then she went back to fit her gown. She was amazed at their speed of doing things in America. It is possible to plan a wedding here in just a week or two, whereas in her country, bridal preparations require at least a year of planning. The wedding would take place at Isabel's parish church in Forest Hills, a decent neighborhood in Queens.

In America, it is the bride who foots the bill for the wedding as depicted in the movie *Father of the Bride*. Not so in the Philippines. The Filipino groom saves and spends for the wedding. In the rural area, prior to the wedding, the groom even works in the farm of the bride's family and does household chores to be in her family's graces. In the urban scene, there have been notable changes in recent years. Some brides now share in the wedding expenses for practical reasons, especially if they are employed.

The anticipation of Isabel's forthcoming wedding put back a little life into Cara. She had been going through her daily activities perfunctorily. She lost her get-up-and-go spirit lately and her appetite for food. Not seeing Daniel and not hearing his voice for a week were taking their toll on her. She had never felt love of this magnitude before. She thought, this must be how it feels to be hit by a bolt of lightning. I'm terrified of lightning. Can love be also terrifying? For an entire week her movements were lifeless. She went home after work forlorn and dejected. She entered her apartment wearily and sat down on her sofa. She was exhausted, yet she did not do much work at the office. Her phone rang and she answered it with a dry 'hello'.

"Cara, it's David. Brace yourself. Daniel has been shot! He's in the hospital. It's in the news. Switch on your TV." Cara's knees began to buckle down from shock. She switched on the TV and Daniel's photo was flashed. The newscaster said that he was undergoing operation at Mount Sinai Hospital. The gunman was apparently a madman and believed to be black, he reported.

"David, is he all right? What happened?," she asked, her voice shaky.

"He was coming out of GCN late this afternoon when the gunman tried to approach him and just shot him. Luckily the gunman was not close enough, but Daniel got it below the shoulder. He lost consciousness when he fell down, and was rushed to the hospital bleeding. They're operating on him now."

"David, I want to see him," she pleaded, starting to cry.

"It may not be a good idea at this time, Cara. The hospital is teeming with reporters. Don't worry, Daniel will pull through. I'll be calling you again. We'll find a way somehow to whisk you inside the hospital, but not at this time, Cara. Take it easy now, okay?"

"Thanks, David. Please update me on his condition."

"I will. Don't worry. I promise to update you regularly."

Cara was distraught. Why did this happen to Daniel? What if he dies?, she questioned. She realized she could not live without him. She went to her bedroom, knelt down before the crucifix at her bedside and prayed.

"Lord, please don't let Daniel die," Cara implored in between tears. She prayed to his guardian angel to watch over him. She cried herself to sleep, worrying about him and feeling completely helpless.

The next morning, Cara woke up with a heaviness in her chest. She was relieved when David called to report on Daniel's condition.

"Daniel is out of danger, Cara. The doctors removed the bullet last night. There's no damage to any vital organ. When he was being wheeled out of the operating room, he was delirious and he was calling your name."

"Has he regained consciousness?"

"Yes, this morning, but he's running a fever now. I'm sure he'll be okay soon. Daniel is a fighter."

"I do want to see him, David."

"I know, Cara, but we'll probably have to wait for a few more days when the reporters disperse. Right now they're waiting there for a scoop, and we don't want you to get involved. You know how they can create stories. Can you hold on a little longer? I promise you I'll find a way. Okay?"

"Okay. Thanks, David." Daniel calling her name? It comforted her.

* * *

Georgia consoled Cara and agreed with David's suggestion that she should not visit Daniel yet at the hospital.

"It's agonizing, Georgia, knowing he's hurt and I'm not there with him. I can't wait to see him."

"I'm sure it won't be for long. Those reporters won't stay there forever if they can see that they have no scoop. You should avoid being seen by them because one picture can tell a story. You know how they can embellish their stories. You better believe it."

"In an earlier newscast, one reporter said that the gunman was black. It turned out to be a wrong assumption because the gunman was a white man. That's being racist."

"I heard that, too. They often associate blacks with crime, my dear."

"That's not fair."

When she got home after work, Cara called Melissa. They talked long about Daniel's critical condition, and her cousin calmed her down.

Chapter

24

On the third day of Daniel's confinement, David called Cara to tell her that it may be safe already to sneak her into Daniel's hospital room. Cara decided to seek Joey's assistance in getting them into the hospital inconspicuously. David and Isabel came to pick her up.

"I don't understand. Why did this man shoot Daniel?," Cara asked.

"You can tell he's deranged. He confessed he wanted to be in the news. He's under police custody now," David replied.

"Are there really people like that?" Cara wanted to know.

"Oh, yes. He admitted that he wanted to shoot either Peter Jennings or Daniel. The guy is really crazy. He had no idea that Peter Jennings had already passed away. Anyway, he waited outside the GCN building. Daniel doesn't usually exit the building at the front, but on this particular afternoon, he decided to walk to the nearby coffeeshop," David explained.

"That gunman has taste. He certainly knows how to pick the good-looking ones," Isabel commented.

"I'm glad Daniel is all right. I was consumed with worry," Cara confessed.

"He kept calling for you, Cara, within everybody's hearing," David revealed to her.

"Who were there?," Cara asked.

"His mom and dad who rushed to the hospital, officemates and friends from GCN, and Madeline too. Even our big boss was there. The network's top management was concerned because Daniel is too valuable to us. The hospital staff, of course. Fortunately, the press was barred from getting in. When he continued asking for you, his mom held his hand and said to him, "Cara will be here, darling," but Daniel didn't seem to be awake yet, just delirious as he was coming out of the operating room. Then the attending doctor asked, 'Who's Cara?', and we just looked at each other. I whispered to him that you're someone special to Daniel."

"I am?," she asked herself audibly, but she was glad that Madeline was there when Daniel called her name. That should put her in her place.

"He loves you, Cara," David confirmed. "He even has your picture on his desk, and everyone in our office unit is aware of his feelings for you."

Cara was perplexed. "I don't recall giving him my picture, David."

"Remember those shots Isabel and I took at his place? He had the one of you smiling enlarged. He has another smaller one with the two of you in his wallet."

"But he hasn't even told me he loves me."

"He's crazy about you. He admitted it to me. He's just extra careful in revealing his feelings too soon because he knows you're different. He also told me about your agreement not to see or call each other for a month, and it's killing him. How do you feel towards him, Cara?"

"I love him, too, David. I was brought up not to be too aggressive when it comes to these things, so I can't just openly tell him how I feel before he has even said anything."

"I agree with you, Cara," Isabel confirmed.

"Now I understand. I do hope the two of you will end up with each other," David said.

"How wonderful. We'll have another wedding," Isabel added.

"By the way, Cara, thanks for forwarding to us those jokes and anecdotes through e-mail. Daniel and I enjoyed them. It was the only thing which made him laugh during your separation," David told her.

"How did you like the computer sayings and lingo?"

"Hilarious. The bible personalities, too."

"David, what happens with *Pulse* when Daniel is not available?," Cara asked.

"We have a back-up interviewer. He's good, but he lacks Daniel's charisma. Daniel is also a hands-on anchor. He formulates the questions himself, and he's adept in asking the right ones."

David drove towards the back door of the hospital where Joey was waiting.

"He's all right, Cara. Luckily, it missed his heart," Joey reported.

Joey led them to the wing where Daniel's room was located, without passing by the nurses' station. After escorting them, Joey left to make his rounds. Daniel was asleep when they reached his room. His mom was in the room with him. She was happy to see Cara and they hugged each other.

"I'm glad you came, Cara. Daniel has been asking for you."

"How is he, Mrs. Devereau?"

"A lot better. He has no more fever, but his wound still has to heal."

Cara sat by Daniel's bedside and watched him lovingly. He was a little pale, his hair was slightly tousled, and he had a three-day-old stubble, but to Cara he was still her handsome prince. After a few minutes, Daniel opened his eyes. When he saw Cara, his face lit up. He uttered her name softly and reached for her hand.

"Are you a dream?" he asked her.

"How are you, Daniel?"

"Much better. I miss you, Cara."

"I miss you, too."

"Really?," he replied with a half-smile. "Aren't you breaking our pact by coming here?" He was trying to tease her.

"This is an emergency, Daniel." Cara answered seriously.

"Maybe I should get shot more often in order to see you?," he kidded her.

"Don't even think of it," she said assertively. "David and Isabel just sneaked me in so I could visit you, but I'm not supposed to stay long. Joey helped us get through without being noticed."

"I'm grateful to them. Joey looked in on me and he told me you were worried about me. Is it true, Cara?"

"Yes, Daniel, I was worried about you." He tightened his grip on her hand.

"I don't know what's more painful, the bullet or not seeing you."

"Oh, Daniel," she reacted, feeling conscious. "I brought you a book to read while you're recuperating. I hope you haven't read this yet." She handed him a copy of *Tuesdays With Morrie*.

"No, not yet. Thank you, Cara. I've heard about this book. I'm sure it's good reading."

"I can imagine the pain you went through, Daniel. It must have been terrible."

"I didn't even notice the gunman because my thoughts were on you, Cara. I walked out of the office aimlessly. I was going out for a cup of coffee after work. I'm just a Muggle, you know, with no magic wand to fend off my attacker." Cara was amused with his comparison to a *Harry Potter* character. "I'm a bleeder, and I lost blood. That must have weakened me."

"I hope you'll regain your strength soon." She gazed at him with pity.

"Thanks for your concern." Then he looked at her tenderly. "When will I see you again?"

"I suppose at David and Isabel's wedding. You're the best man, remember? Will you be strong enough by then?"

"I won't miss it for the world. Thank you for coming to visit me, Cara. It means a lot to me. You're my best medicine."

"Please get well soon, Daniel." She planted a kiss on his forehead. He held on to her hand for some time, reluctant to release it.

They left Daniel's room with David leading the way to the backdoor where they came in. Cara felt momentary happiness after seeing Daniel. It was a relief to know that he was on the road to recovery.

Chapter

25

"Cara, it's Vince. I'll be in New York tomorrow to attend a convention of orthopedic surgeons." It was her brother calling from Chicago.

"Vince! That's wonderful. When can I see you?"

"It's a two-day convention, but I'm free tomorrow evening, so we can have dinner."

"That's great. I miss you, Vince."

"I miss you, too, Cara. I'll call you when I get there."

Vince and Cara had an ideal brother-sister relationship. He played his big brother role to the hilt, being several years older than Cara. He acted as a second parent to Cara and chaperoned her to parties. When Vince took a Filipino wife last year in Chicago, Cara could not come to the wedding because she could not get leave from her work, so she had not yet met his wife Nina. Their parents flew to Chicago to attend the wedding. Nina worked as a pediatrician at the same hospital where Vince had his practice.

Vince called Cara the following day.

"Cara, I'm now in New York. I'm staying at the Essex House. Where do you want to go for dinner tonight?"

"I have a better idea. Why don't I just cook dinner for us at my place? I'd like to talk to you longer, and we'll have more privacy. Is that okay with you?"

"Sure. Don't take too much trouble, Cara. A simple meal will do. I'll be there at seven."

Like Cara, Vince loved pasta. She prepared a vegetable casserole and a pasta dish. He did not have a sweet tooth, so she concocted a fruit salad sweetened with fruit juice. Vince arrived on the dot. When he hugged Cara, she realized how much she longed for the warmth and comfort of a hug from a loved one. She clung to him.

"Cara, I sense something is wrong."

"I had a tough week, Vince, and I've been feeling low. I'm glad you're here because I need you now." Vince embraced her tightly, and it was comforting to Cara.

"Does this have anything to do with Daniel Devereaux?" He looked at her straight in the eye, but Cara did not say a word. "I heard in the news about the shooting. Is he okay?"

"He's recovering. After the National Inquirer article came out, I suggested that we don't keep in touch with each other, and not seeing him is painful. Then he got shot. I visited him at the hospital. I love him, Vince, and I miss him very much." She started to cry.

"Ssh," he tried to calm her and rocked her in his arms. "How well do you know him, Cara?"

"Well enough. We've gone out several times. He's a wonderful man, Vince."

"Does he love you?"

"We haven't actually said 'I love you' to each other yet. He respects me, and that's what is important to me."

"Oh, Cara. What can I say to you? I haven't even met the man. My only concern is you. I don't want to see you get hurt. At the moment, maybe you need a change of scene. Why don't you come to Chicago with me for the weekend? I'll take care of your plane fare. You've never been to Chicago, and it's about time you meet Nina. You'll like her."

"What about my work?"

"We'll fly Friday evening, and you can fly back Sunday afternoon, so you won't miss work. I'll request the hotel to make the travel arrangements. How about it?"

"It sounds okay. Thanks, Vince. I guess I need the diversion."

"I'm meeting Joey tomorrow afternoon. Do you want to come along?"

"Maybe I should leave you two alone. You have a lot of catching up to do."

* * *

Cara decided to call David to ask about Daniel.

"Hi, David. It's Cara. How is Daniel?"

"He checked out of the hospital today, Cara. He's now recuperating in Long Island where his mom can pamper him."

"He hates that, but I guess he needs pampering in his present condition."

"Sure he does."

How Cara wished she could be the one to pamper him.

"My brother is taking me to Chicago with him for the weekend. He's here to attend a convention. I may check with you on Daniel's condition when I get back."

"Sure, Cara. Enjoy yourself."

"Thanks, David. Give my love to Isabel."

* * *

Vince and Cara talked for the duration of their flight to Chicago. Their conversation centered on family and their respective work. They had not seen each other face to face for years since Vince left for the U.S.

"Joey seems to have a good impression of Daniel Devereaux," he told her.

"He does? But they met only briefly."

"Well, he thinks the guy is serious with you. You know, Joey still has feelings for you, Cara."

"Doesn't he have a girlfriend? He denied it to me when I asked him."

"He wants a Filipina, and he wants someone like you."

"What's this with you Filipino guys? Why do you always prefer Filipinas?"

When they arrived in Vince's condo in downtown Chicago, Nina was already home. Nina was a Filipino beauty, slim like Cara, but smaller in stature. She was pleasant and soft-spoken. Cara observed that she was devoted to Vince.

"Cara, we meet finally," Nina said as they greeted each other. "You look like Vince." Vince and Cara had the same 'smiling' and expressive eyes, inherited from their mother, which crinkled when they smiled.

"That's a compliment. I have a handsome brother," Cara replied. Vince was visibly pleased. "Did you know that Vince was popular with the women back home?"

"So I've heard," Nina replied with a smile. "Am I lucky."

"You've got a nice place here, and it's right in the hub," Cara commented.

"The size is still all right for us even if we have a child," Vince said.

"We're planning to start a family by next year, Cara," Nina added.

"That's wonderful," Cara reacted. "I'll be an aunt then."

"In the future, we'll start looking for a house in the suburbs, somewhere in Evanston or Lake Forest," Vince explained.

"I took a leave from the hospital, Cara, so I can take you around Chicago," Nina said.

"You didn't have to do that, Nina."

"It's all right. I haven't gone on leave for some time anyway. Where do you want to go tomorrow?"

"This is my first time in Chicago, so everything is new to me. Maybe I should see the Sears Tower, being a Chicago landmark. Can we go to Michael Jordan's restaurant?"

"Of course, you're a Michael Jordan fan." Vince smiled in remembrance. "I sent you a copy of his book, didn't I?"

"Yes, thanks for that."

The next day, Nina and Cara toured Chicago. It was as cold as New York, but it was extremely windy at this time of the year. They went up the Sears Tower, browsed around the plush shops downtown, and had lunch at Michael Jordan's restaurant. It was too much to expect that she would see Michael Jordan there, but she was hoping. They also dropped by St. John's Hospital because Cara wanted to see their place of work. Vince had no surgery that day, so he was able to join them for coffee at the hospital cafeteria.

Vince made reservations for dinner at a classy restaurant serving continental cuisine in downtown Chicago. Cara liked the ambience, and the food excellent. Cara missed her family, so the time spent with Vince and Nina was precious to her. The following day was Sunday, and they attended Mass in the morning. Vince did not go to the hospital, and he drove them to the suburbs of Chicago where they had lunch in a quaint restaurant with a scenic view of Lake Michigan.

In the afternoon, Vince and Nina drove Cara to O'Hare Airport for her flight to New York. Cara hated partings, and she knew she was going to miss them.

"Thank you very much for everything. I had a great weekend with you two," she told Vince and Nina.

"You should come again, Cara, and stay longer next time," Nina said.

"That would be nice."

"And next time we want to meet Daniel," Vince told her.

"I promise."

* * *

When Cara got back to New York, she had an e-mail from Daniel. It said: *Beloved Cara, I heard you went to Chicago with your brother. I would have wanted to meet him. I hope you had a good visit. I'm getting stronger everyday, with Mom's attention, and can now use my laptop to send e-mail. I'm spending a lot of time with Dad, sometimes just talking. I've ventured outside the house up to the yard and played with Fudge. I enjoyed reading 'Tuesdays With Morrie'. It's an inspiring book and it may even become my Bible. I'm still missing you a lot. Love, Daniel'.*

"Daniel, you made my day," Cara said to herself aloud. She sat in front of her laptop and answered Daniel's e-mail: *Dear Daniel, I'm glad to know that you're getting better. I pray for you everyday. I had a great time in Chicago with Vince and Nina. I missed Vince. He wanted to meet you, too. It was my first time in Chicago. I was hoping I'd see*

Michael Jordan, but he was not at his restaurant when we had lunch there. I miss you, too. Get well soon. Best, Cara.

Daniel was amused with her reference to Michael Jordan. His mom caught him smiling.

"It's good to see you smile, son. Is it good news?"

"It's from Cara."

"I'm glad you're communicating."

"I miss her, Mom."

"I suppose she misses you, too, darling."

"She says she does," he told his mom, looking quite pleased.

* * *

Cara and Melissa met in downtown Manhattan for pizza when she got back from Chicago.

"How was your trip?", Melissa asked.

"It was fun and I had a nice time with Vince and Nina. They're a happy couple. I like Nina, and she's the right partner for Vince."

"Cara, you've lost weight, I notice. Does this have something to do with Daniel and you."

"Yes, Melissa. His getting shot and our separation have taken their toll on me. I've lost my appetite, and I keep thinking of him. I love him, but I'm not sure of his feelings for me."

"He loves you, trust me. Aren't you going see him at his friend David's wedding"

"Yes, he's best man."

"Well, think positive and expect something good from this encounter."

"I hope so. Just the thought of seeing him again excites me."

Melissa always managed to make Cara feel better.

Chapter

26

On the morning of the wedding day, Cara took the subway to Forest Hills with a small valise. Earlier, Isabel brought home Cara's gown and told her to go to Forest Hills early so she would have plenty of time to prepare herself and dress up at her place. The wedding was scheduled in the afternoon. She reached Isabel's home late morning and joined her family for lunch. It gave her ample time to meet their close-knit family. The members of Isabel's family were all friendly, and they made her feel at home. Their closeness reminded Cara of her own family.

Isabel's color motif was soft pink. The gowns of the female bridal participants were identical, embellished with dainty lace and seed pearls of the same pink shade. Isabel's own gown was lovely with a defined bodice of white lace. She epitomized the beautiful bride. Cara experienced a wave of excitement as she put on her gown, which showed off her slim figure. She looked at her face in the mirror and noticed that her cheekbones were more prominent now due to her weight loss. Will Daniel like how she looks?, she asked herself.

In church before the ceremony, she appeared more nervous than the bride. When it was Cara's turn to walk towards the altar, she saw David from afar standing in wait with Daniel beside him. Daniel's eyes never left her and followed her to where she stopped and stood. When she reached her assigned spot, she turned her head in his direction and she saw Daniel still looking at her intently with a hint of a smile on his face. She noticed that he had lost a little weight from his ordeal. He looked dashing in his toxedo.

Cara loved weddings. To her, a wedding is a celebration of love which brings out the welcome mat to a lifetime of intimacy and sharing. She told herself, it must be wonderful to marry one's soul mate with whom you can laugh, cry, and feel, to whom you can open up your heart and unravel your innermost dreams. She believed that together the husband and wife can nurture their relationship through a deep commitment to making each other happy. Marriage is an enhancer, an enriching experience where each party becomes a better person because of the other. She dreamed of her own wedding day. She pictured herself reciting her vows to the man she promised to love and cherish. In her imagination, the groom's face was Daniel's.

David and Isabel's wedding was one happy event, a culmination of a two-year courtship. David was not Catholic, but he agreed to a Catholic ceremony for the sake of Isabel and her family. The lively reception afterwards echoed their vow of love for each other where their respective families and friends shared in their happiness.

Cara found herself seated next to Daniel. David and Isabel must have maneuvered the seating arrangement. Daniel greeted her with a kiss on the cheek.

"You look stunning, Cara. I couldn't take my eyes off you."

"Thank you, Daniel. You look good yourself in a tuxedo. Are you fully recovered?," she asked with concern in her voice.

"More or less. There's still a slight pain, but I'm managing."

"You seemed to have lost weight."

"You, too, I notice. You're still beautiful, Cara. Why did you lose weight?"

Cara could not answer him and she tried to avoid his eyes.

"Does it have anything to do with missing me?" He was in a teasing mood.

She glanced at him and he was smiling engagingly at her with a twinkle in his eyes. Before she could say anything, the band started to play *Moonlight Serenade.*

"They're playing our music." He stood up, took her hand, and led her to the dance floor where David and Isabel were already dancing with each other. The parents and other relatives and friends joined in.

On the dance floor, Cara unwittingly put her left hand on Daniel's shoulder, unconscious of his wound, and he winced.

"Oh, I'm so sorry, Daniel. Does it hurt?," Cara asked, much worried. "I'm okay," he assured her. He took her hand and kissed it, caressing it with his lips while looking into her eyes, and once more Cara felt a ripple of desire. Then he drew her to him in a tight tender embrace, and she knew this was where she belonged, in Daniel's arms. He kissed her hair and her temple, then her forehead. When she raised her face towards his, he brought down his lips on hers abruptly, savoring her luscious lips, then stopped just as abruptly, wreaking havoc on Cara's emotional equilibrium.

"Oh, Cara, what are you doing to me?," he whispered into her ear, his voice full of passion. In moments like this, Cara could only be silent. How she longed to tell him that she loved him, but she was afraid to seize the moment and initiate it. When they returned to their table holding hands after the music, Cara was still in a stupor.

"How did you get here, by the way? I wanted to ask you earlier but our no-contact agreement crossed my mind. GCN assigned a car and driver to me so I don't have to drive," he said.

"I took the subway this morning. Isabel wanted me to come early so I could dress up here."

"I'll take you home. We'll stop by my place first. There's something very important which can't wait. Is that all right with you?"

"It's okay, I guess."

"I promise I won't seduce you. Scout's honor," he demonstrated with the two- finger scout sign. It brought a smile to Cara's face. He was teasing her again. She enjoyed this type of banter between them as it unveiled new facets of their individual characters, and lent a certain degree of intimacy to their relationship.

The dancing gathered beat and everybody was on the dance floor, mostly from Isabel's South American progeny, including the children. Isabel's brother Juan approached Cara and asked her to dance the *rumba* with him. Juan was quite a dancer, guiding Cara expertly. Daniel watched, never taking his eyes away from Cara, admiring the way she danced gracefully and loving her smile.

"I didn't know you dance well," Daniel commented after she sat down.

"You still have a lot to know about me, Daniel." It was her turn to tease.

Then the band played a Sinatra tune, and Daniel rose from his seat.

"Will you dance the fox trot with me?," he asked her. Cara was surprised because she did not know he could dance the fox trot.

"What about your shoulder?"

"I'll manage. Don't worry."

They glided and dipped to *You Make Me Feel So Young*. Cara loved the fox trot, and Daniel was a smooth dancer.

"Why, Daniel, you're a revelation."

"You've a lot to know about me, too, Cara."

As best man, Daniel offered a toast to the newlyweds. He delivered a brief speech extolling David's good qualities as a person, friend, and co-worker. He assured Isabel that David would make an ideal husband, and wished the couple a lifetime of happiness. After Daniel had returned to his seat, David unexpectedly grabbed the microphone and requested him to sing a song, catching Daniel by surprise.

"Another one of David's bright ideas," Daniel reacted.

"Come on, Daniel, show them," Cara urged him.

"I don't think I can get out of this. It's the groom's request." He stood up and looked at Cara. "This one's for you."

Daniel went up front again and sang *She* from the movie *Notting Hill*. Cara could only swoon privately as he sang it with much feeling. She was oblivious of the people around her and mesmerized by his singing. He focused solely on her, and the words and meaning of the song suffused her being. Daniel received a deserved applause, especially from the GCN crowd present.

The merriment lasted for hours. When they said goodbye to David and Isabel, David took Daniel aside.

"Hey, pal, you better make your move with Cara. She loves you. She admitted it to me and Isabel when we visited you at the hospital."

"She did?," Daniel replied grinning.

"She's not about to make the first move, so you better do something about it fast."

"I plan to do that." "Good," David said, pressing his good shoulder. "I'll talk to you when we get back from our honeymoon. You should start making plans."

"I will."

Chapter

27

Daniel was silent during their ride to Manhattan. He held Cara's hand the whole time.

"Daniel, you're so quiet. Does your shoulder hurt?," she asked in a concerned tone, and he was touched.

"I'm all right, just deep in thought," he assured her, and kissed her hand.

They were cruising along Manhattan when the driver slowed down.

"We're here," Daniel said. He alighted from the car and helped Cara, who made a quick survey of the surroundings.

"Daniel, this is the Empire State Building. Why are we here?

"I've something to show you."

They took the elevator up to the view deck. The number of visitors was dwindling at this late hour. Still in their wedding attire, they merited a second look. Daniel led her by the hand to a private spot. Cara was feeling nervous, and she felt her heart beating faster than usual. Daniel suddenly took out a small velvet box from his pocket, then handed it to Cara, looking deeply into her eyes.

"What's this? Aren't you early for Christmas?" She smiled innocently, but a wave of confusion swept over her.

"Open it," he told her. Slowly, Cara opened the box.

"Oh, my gosh!," she uttered softly, staring in amazement at what was inside it.

There lay the most exquisite heart-shaped diamond ring she had ever seen, done in simple setting. She continued to stare at it speechless as it glittered in her hand. Then she cast an inquiring look at Daniel beside her.

"It's beautiful. Daniel, what does this mean?," she asked him almost in a whisper.

"I'm asking you to marry me, Cara." He looked at her lovingly, taking her hand in his.

"You're proposing to me?," she asked him in a nervous and unsteady voice. She could not believe what she was hearing.

"Yes. I want you to be my wife."

"I don't know what to say." She put one hand in her chest as if to still her heart.

"A 'yes' would be perfect, and I won't accept any other answer. I love you, Cara. I love you very much. I know you love me, and I want to hear you say it."

"How did you know?"

"A little bird told me," he answered her with a smile. He could still tease. She knew it was David. Tears welled in Cara's eyes.

"Cara, darling, what is it? Is it something I said?," he asked her tenderly, touching her hair in a loving gesture. He took out his handkerchief and wiped the single teardrop which started to slide down her cheek.

"Oh, Daniel, I've wanted to hear you say that you love me." She waited so long for his declaration of love that hearing Daniel say it made her eyes water.

"Is that the reason for the tears?," he asked with an amused expression. "I'll say it a million times if you want me to," he said in the gentlest tone. "I'll even shout it from the top of this building."

"I didn't expect you to ask me to marry you. I just thought …"

He interrupted her. "I'm asking you now, Cara. Marry me." This was more than Cara had dreamed of. She had only hoped he would ask her to be his girlfriend. She thought that was where their relationship was leading to.

"Daniel, did you think this over carefully? You know we're worlds apart, and I don't want to complicate your life." Her face mirrored a fragment of her concern.

"We have so much in common, Cara. It's true we're two separate beings from two different worlds, but we can be partners in the real sense. Don't you find that exciting? Marriage is a miracle, darling. The two of us can make it happen. Despite our cultural differences, we're compatible, and that's a good start."

"But the entire time we were seeing each other, there was no talk of love."

"You don't know how many times I was tempted to bare my heart to you, but I had to be very sure you feel the same way. I wanted to do it right and at the proper time."

"Are you certain this is what you want, Daniel?"

"Absolutely! I've never been so sure of anything in my entire life. I've never met anyone like you, and I've never said 'I love you' to any woman before. In the past, I always ended up feeling that something was missing in my life. I know now it's you, Cara, and you're the only woman I truly love. You said before that you want to marry your soul mate. I'm your soul mate." he told her convincingly.

Daniel then drew her to him tightly and kissed her wildly until she felt limp with uncontrollable emotions. Her heart was thumping fast like Gene Krupa on his drums. He was that famous drummer in the sixties whom her father liked.

"Now, do you believe me?," Daniel asked her with raw passion in his eyes.

"Oh, Daniel, I love you so much," she responded, returning his kisses with equal intensity. He yearned to hear those very words from her lips. He was overjoyed with the way she reciprocated and finally acknowledged her feelings for him openly.

"That's exactly what I want to hear from you, darling. I can't wait any longer. I want to wake up every morning with you beside me. I want to grow old with you, and spend the rest of my life with you. Even if these are cliches, they're real to me. I've waited for you all my life." Then he went down on one knee. "Will you marry me, Cara?"

"You don't have to do that, Daniel. Please get up. There are still people around," she told him smiling.

"Say 'yes' and I will." he said, almost pleading.

She looked at him with tenderness. This is the man I love with my whole heart, and now he wants me to be part of his world. I can't ask for anything more, she told herself.

Yes, Daniel. I want to be your wife more than anything else."

"Yes!" He rose jubilantly with a clenched fist and a wide grin. "I'm the happiest man alive." He slipped the ring into her finger, then kissed her long and hard.

"I heard there's something special to you about the Empire State Building, that's why I decided to propose to you here," he told her.

"Oh, Daniel, it's very romantic."

Chapter

28

Daniel knew they needed a private moment to talk about a lot of things and make plans. He asked the driver to proceed to his place and park while he took Cara up to his condo. As he unlocked the door and led her inside, the aura of his place exuded an unexplainable warmth, which was comforting to Cara. Is this a good omen?, she wondered.

They settled on the sofa and continued to kiss and caress each other until they were out of breath. Then she relaxed in his embrace, the top of her head resting on his chin.

"Daniel, this is the perfect engagement ring." She held up her left hand to admire the ring on her finger. "You have great taste."

"Well, I had the right adviser who happens to know you well. I asked her to accompany me to Tiffany's, and she knew exactly what you wanted."

"Melissa?" He nodded his head.

"She knows me all right, and we window-shopped at Tiffany's recently. I can't believe she kept this a secret from me."

"In the car on our way here, I was quiet because I was thinking about what I'd do if you turn me down. I vowed I'd do everything in my power to make you mine, Cara."

"Daniel Devereaux, how can you talk like that when you can have any woman you want?"

"You're the only woman I want, and I wasn't sure you'd want me."

"You're the man of my dreams, Daniel, but I had my apprehensions. Didn't my being …you know, not Caucasian, bother you at all?"

"Not for a moment, dearest. It didn't even cross my mind. What bothered me was that you might prefer someone from your own country, like our ex-boyfriend Joey, and I was tortured by that."

"Joey and I are just friends now. Oh, Daniel, I should be the one feeling jealous with all the women in your life. I'm sure you've broken many hearts."

"Is that what you think? I don't know about that, but if I ever did, it was not deliberate. You're the only woman that matters to me now. I didn't even date anyone else after I met you. My quest for the right woman ended with you, Cara."

She felt wonderful hearing such words from him. "What do you love about me, Daniel? I'm curious."

"I love everything about you, darling. I love your smile most of all, your exuberance, and your sense of humor. I'm happy when I'm with you. You're always your natural self, and there's nothing put-on about you. You're intelligent that talking to you is sheer pleasure. You're principled and virtuous. You're extraordinary, Cara, do you know that?"

"Virtuous? Oh, no. If my parents find out that I indulged in passionate kissing with someone who wasn't even my fiance, I'll surely be sternly reprimanded." It made Daniel laugh.

"When did you realize that you love me?," she asked him.

"I must have loved you the moment I laid eyes on you. I was charmed by your smile when we were first introduced. I was my usual lackadaisical self that morning, and suddenly there you were. You invaded my thoughts after that because we kept bumping into each other. I was glad when you later told me you're 25 because I thought you were very young then. When I discovered how kind and wonderful you are, my feelings for you became even stronger. How about you, darling, when did you start loving me?"

"When you kissed me. That was when I knew for certain that I love you. You taught me how to feel as a woman. I loved you even more when you respected my womanhood. I was physically attracted to you the first time we were introduced when you looked at me deeply with those green eyes that seemed to reach my soul. You were very handsome, but I found you frightening then."

"You mean, I was like an ogre?," he inquired half-jokingly.

"It's not that. You were intensely masculine, it was intimidating. I even thought you were arrogant the first time we met because you didn't smile."

"Well, you made me smile." He played with her hair while cradling her in his arms and she liked it.

"It drove me crazy when you started responding to my kisses because then I knew that I could ignite the fire in you," he confessed. "I had to control myself when I kissed you because I was conscious of the values you espouse, but then I couldn't stop myself from kissing you. Where did you learn how to kiss back like that, huh?" He was teasing and probing at the same time.

"From you, of course. I'm totally lost when you kiss me, Daniel, and I just follow my feelings." He seemed satisfied with her answer. "When we agreed not to see or call each other, I was missing you terribly and I was like a zombie at work. I lost weight just from thinking of you."

"I was feeling miserable, too. You can ask David. I had this constant fear of losing you in the absence of any commitment between us. I was insanely jealous of Joey. I was afraid that the two of you would go back to each other and I'd lose you completely. I could see that he's still cares for you, Cara."

"There will always be a special bond between Joey and me. I still love him, but not in the same way that I love you. I told him the first time we saw each other again that I have feelings for you and he wished me happiness. Maybe, just maybe, if Joey and I had found each other before I met you, it's possible that we could have gotten back together. But it didn't happen that way, Daniel, because then I had already met you, and you had captured my heart."

"Thank God for destiny. You know, we should be grateful to Alec for giving you that assignment with us. Otherwise, I don't know how our paths could have crossed in a city as big as New York. I dread to think that if we hadn't met, you'd probably be back with Joey. He knew you first."

"My relationship with Joey in the past was never like this, darling. We just shared a certain kind of primordial affinity from knowing each other since we were children. He's like a brother to me now. When we kissed before, it wasn't like what you and I have and feel now."

"You mean, like this?" He smothered her with kisses until she pushed him away gently, gasping. Daniel drew her back to him.

"Do you realize you just called me 'darling'? That makes me happy. Come here." He sat her in his lap. "That's okay. Stop me when I get carried away, otherwise we won't be able to think clearly. I promise to make you happy, Cara. Will you be happy living here with me after we're married?"

"I'll be happy anywhere with you, Daniel." She snuggled up to him.

"I'll take care of you, my love," he promised her.

"No, I'll take care of you. I'll cook your meals, attend to your clothes and needs, *palangga*." She uttered the last word lovingly.

"What did you just call me?"

"*Palangga*. It's the southern word for 'beloved' in my country. It's a common term of endearment there which my mother calls me sometimes."

He tried to say the word, but he sounded awkward, and Cara could not help but giggle.

"You're making fun of me," he scolded her.

"No, it's just that you're so cute." She kissed the tip of his nose.

"Daniel, I want to have your children, and I hope one of them will have your green eyes."

"How many are we planning to have?" He was back to teasing her.

"As many as you want."

"We'll have our honeymoon first, love. Where do you want to go for our honeymoon?"

"It doesn't matter. I just want to be with you." She convinced him with a loving look, which moved him.

"There must be a particular place you want to visit."

"Well, there was a time I wanted to go to Florence to see the statue of David."

"Why do you want to see a naked statue, huh?," he kidded her.

"Daniel, it's a work of art! When Vince and I were in our teens, Papa brought us to Italy to meet our relatives, but we didn't have time to go to Florence. I also want to see the *aurora borealis*, the northern lights."

"We can arrange that, but these will all come later. Right after our wedding, I want to be in seclusion with you, away from the outside world. I want to explore every inch of you. We still have so much to discover in each other."

"Uh-huh. You're right. I don't know everything about you. How do I know you don't turn into a werewolf during full moon?…or you can be a serial killer!" She pretended to be terrified, but his earlier statement excited her.

Daniel let out a hearty laugh. "Suppose I am, what are you going to do about it, huh?," he said, pinching her cheek in a playful manner. "You may also have a tattoo somewhere in that beautiful body of yours that I don't know of."

"Maybe," she answered in a naughty manner.

"Nah, you're not the type. Well, do you want to spend your honeymoon initially at the Waldorf with the werewolf?"

"Whatever you want," she laughed in return. Then suddenly she extricated herself from his embrace.

"Daniel, we're forgetting something."

"What?" He sounded alarmed.

"The pre-nuptial agreement!"

"I won't allow that, Cara. Never!" There was a trace of anger in his voice.

"But there may be talks," she explained in a soft tone, sensing his altered mood.

"I don't like putting restrictions on marriage. I believe in sharing as the cornerstone of an ideal relationship. You can't attach a price tag on love, Cara. When we marry, we belong to each other, and that goes with what we have and own," he told her emphatically.

"I just don't want to get you into any more trouble."

"That's between you and me, and that's final," he stated firmly.

Cara knew that was the end of the subject. These were among the characteristics she admired in Daniel. He was strong and decisive, and now he was already exercising his headship over her. When he sensed that she honored his decision, his tone changed.

"There's something we can do together. I earn more than enough, so you can help me channel a portion of it for worthy causes," he suggested to her.

"You're so kind, Daniel. How can I not love you? There's a lot we can do for others," hugging him tighter.

"Let's work on that when we get settled, okay?"

"Okay. *Palangga*, there's something I want to do now," she said.

"What's that?"

"I want to run my fingers through your hair. I've always wanted to do that."

"Go ahead. I'm yours," he responded, delighted with her simple request.

"Oh, Daniel, it's impossible for me to look at you and not love you," she told him with much affection, while running her fingers through his lush brown hair, then raining little kisses on his face.

"Cara, darling," he reacted, unleashing his feelings with a passionate kiss on her lips, then drawing back. "Dearest, the reason I asked the driver to wait was because I was afraid of the consequences of bringing you here to my place, and I want to be sure you get home in one piece," he said laughing and embracing her all at once.

"Suppose I don't want you to stop?," she replied mischievously.

"Cara, don't tempt me," he warned her, but the desire was evident in his eyes.

"I only learned how to tease from you," she reasoned out playfully.

"Cara, my beloved, you never cease to amaze me. You're incredible." Daniel was completely captivated by Cara's charm. "Darling, we'll get married right away. I want you to be Mrs. Daniel Devereaux before the new year comes around."

It came as a loving command. She knew this was the man to whom she was ready to submit herself and with whom she wanted to share her every moment.

"Oh, Daniel, there's nothing in the world I want more. I want to be part of your life." They basked in that shared happy moment marked with love and laughter.

Daniel and Cara were fully aware that finding the right partner and being the right partner are what it takes to make the miracle in marriage happen. They knew that no differences in their worlds can stand in the way of their great love for each other.

# # #

About the Author

Cristina Monro is a penname the author uses when writing fiction. The author is a Filipino who shuttles between the Philippines and Singapore. She is an editor, writer, and English instructor. She has a post-graduate Diploma in Language and Literacy Education from the University of the Philippines, and a Bachelor of Arts degree, major in English, from Xavier University. She earned a Certificate for Teaching English as a Second/Foreign Language from De La Salle University. She also completed the Program for Development Managers at the Asian Institute of Management and the Secretarial course at Maryknoll College.

She earlier received a Fellowship Grant from the US-Asia Environmental Partnership and observed the environmental programs of the US and Canada. In the Philippines, she worked for a number of years with San Miguel Corporation, Pilipinas Shell, and Accenture Philippines as Editor, and received several awards from the Public Relations Society of the Philippines in recognition of her work.

She is an author of three published books and co-authored a textbook on Communication Arts. Her hobbies include oil painting of landscapes and still life, mosaic art, patchwork quilting, embroidery, playing the piano and the guitar, and solving crossword puzzles.

Printed in the United States
By Bookmasters